Robert Waters

William Shakespeare Portrayed By Himself

A revelation of the poet in the career and character of one of his own dramatic

heroes

Robert Waters

William Shakespeare Portrayed By Himself
A revelation of the poet in the career and character of one of his own dramatic heroes

ISBN/EAN: 9783337214128

Printed in Europe, USA, Canada, Australia, Japan

Cover: Foto ©Raphael Reischuk / pixelio.de

More available books at **www.hansebooks.com**

WILLIAM SHAKESPEARE

PORTRAYED BY HIMSELF:

A

REVELATION OF THE POET

IN THE CAREER AND CHARACTER OF ONE
OF HIS OWN DRAMATIC HEROES.

By ROBERT WATERS,

AUTHOR OF A "LIFE OF WILLIAM COBBETT," ETC.

" Sadly I survive,
To mock the expectation of the world,
To frustrate prophecies, and to raze out
Rotten opinion, who hath writ me down
After my seeming."

NEW YORK:
WORTHINGTON COMPANY,
747 BROADWAY.

WILLIAM SHAKESPEARE

Portrayed by Himself.

CHAPTER I.

THE UNIVERSAL INTEREST IN THE PERSONALITY OF THE POET—WHAT THE WRITER INTENDS TO SHOW.

IT is said that ten thousand different essays, pamphlets and books have been printed and published concerning the life and writings of William Shakespeare. This is something unparalleled in the history of literature. No other name among men of letters has created such an interest. What an amazing attraction, what a boundless fascination, must people find in the life and character of this man! Men of every nation, of every rank, are captivated by him. All the world wish to know the antecedents, the family, the training, of the man who produced the most superb dramas in literature—whence he derived that marvellous power of dramatic presentation, that wonderful skill, knowledge, and wisdom, as poet, philosopher, and dramatist, which he displays in all his works. All men are amazed at the circumstance, that a man of the people, of no particular education, of no remarkable lineage, should have surpassed all other men in intellectual power, in the richness and greatness of his productions ;—all men, I say, except a few erratic individuals in recent years, whose extraordinary views are not supported by any foundation worth a moment's consideration. People of foreign nations are so much interested in him, that they learn English merely to read his works in the original ; and there is hardly a language capable of literary expression into which these works have not been again and again translated. He is called the father of German literature, and even at the present day is more read and studied in Germany than any native author. His birthplace, now the property of the English nation, has become a Mecca to which pilgrims from the four corners of the world resort ; the relation and explanation of the events of his life form one of the great problems of modern times ; and societies for the study and elucidation of his writings have been organized in every part of the civilized world. He is the glory of the English-speaking race, and every member of that race, from one end of the world to the other, is more or less indebted to him for what he is, for what culture or enlightenment he possesses, for what largeness of view, superior power of expression, or increased social and intellectual advantages, he enjoys ;—indeed, I may say that mankind is indebted to him for a richer and more copious speech, a larger social and intellectual life, and a more abundant fund of rational amusement, than it ever possessed before.

Such is the man whom I propose to unveil, as delineating his own character and career in the person of one of his dramatic heroes ; such is the man whose

life I intend to unfold to my readers,
without the aid of a cipher or any remarkable hocus-pocus, in such plain characters
that all the world may read and perceive
its truth. When the life and character
of a literary man cannot be found in
the records of his friends and acquaintances, and no personal memoirs of him
are extant, the only proper place to look
for him is in his works ; and when the
known incidents of his career, and the
known traits of his character, agree in a
remarkable manner with those of one,
and only one, of his heroes, it is natural
to infer that he delineated himself in that
hero, and that that delineation must
afford a better view of him than any
other that can be obtained. I shall show
that in the very plays in which that
extraordinary gentleman, Mr. Ignatius
Donnelly, has discovered a cipher showing that they were written by Lord Bacon, the real author, Shakespeare, reveals
himself, his life, his character, as plainly
and purposely as any author ever reveal-

show that the identity of this character with the Poet holds good through three different plays ; nay, through four different plays ; and to the man who wishes to make some personal acquaintance with Shakespeare, this presentation of him will, I am confident, afford much more satisfaction, and give a far better view of the man, than any or all of his meager biographies. So sure am I of this, that I think every lover of Shakespeare will, after reading this essay, not only peruse the plays in question with increased satisfaction and delight, but experience a feeling of thankfulness toward the writer for having rescued our beloved Poet from even a suspicion of foul play, and for having silenced forever this vain and pernicious babble about Bacon's authorship of his plays.

CHAPTER II.

SOMETIMES a truth is disco
by long years of labor and p
tudy; sometimes by an unexp
ash of thought. In the latter cas
nvestigation and proof follow the
overy; in the former, they prece
had taken up Huth's " Life of I
Thomas Buckle "—which is a goo
ount of a remarkable man, for
haracter and genius I entertai
eepest respect, and over whos
imely fate I have shed tears of re
nd was running over it for the s
me, when I came to this p
uoted to show the wide scope an
lity of Buckle's talents:

Hear him but reason in divinity,
And, all-admiring, with an inward wish

You would desire the king were made a prelate :
Hear him debate of commonwealth affairs,
You would say, it hath been all-in-all his study :
List his discourse of war, and you shall hear
A fearful battle rendered you in music :
Turn him to any cause of policy,
The Gordian knot of it he will unloose,
Familiar as his garter ; that, when he speaks,
The air, a chartered libertine, is still,
And the mute wonder lurketh in men's ears,
To steal his sweet and honey'd sentences.

On reading this, I said to myself, "That can suit no man except Shakespeare himself : whence are these lines?" On looking up the passage, I found it formed part of the Archbishop's description of Prince Henry, now become king, in the First Act of *King Henry the Fifth ;* and I made up my mind, from that instant, that the character was none other than that of Shakespeare himself. I knew what Prince Henry was, and knew something of him as Henry the Fifth ; but had not, till then, dreamt of him as other than an historical character. Now, the more carefully I studied Shakespeare's portraiture of him, the more I became convinced that the character was a portrait of the Poet himself; and if the reader will have the patience to follow me for a few pages, I hope to convince him likewise of its truth.

From all that we know of Shakespeare's early history, that of Prince Henry corresponds to it very closely; and from all that we know of his later history, the correspondence will be found to be, in a sense, equally close. The character, companions, and habits of life of Prince Henry were such as are known to have been those of the youthful Shakespeare; and the character, companions, and habits of his later years were such as correspond with those of the triumphant and all-surpassing English Poet. We know that Shakespeare was a roysterer in his early days; that his "youth had wandered faulty and irregular"; that he loved good cheer, merry companions, and a free and easy life; that he was fond of lively conversation and wit-combats, and that he excelled in these; that he got into trouble in one, at least, of his escapades with these companions, and that, like the Prince, he suffered at the hands of judicial authority. In fact, the Poet could hardly avoid perceiving these remarkable coincidences, and could hardly avoid recalling his own experiences while delineating those of the Prince. The Prince having been such a man as he had been in his youth ; his experiences and diversions having been similar to his own ; his companions and adventures having been of a like nature, it was natural that he should at once make up his mind to delineate his own character and companions, his own life and adventures, in those of the Prince.

Under these circumstances, the conclusion inevitably forces itself upon the mind, that the Poet, in writing a play in which this character is a leading personage, drew upon his own experience, and painted himself in this character. As this has been done by so many others, is there anything more natural than that he too should, in a work of art, have availed himself of this privilege ?

and is there anything surprising in the fact, that the characters he here drew should be among the most life-like, most interesting and strongest ever drawn by him? Is there anything more natural than that one of these characters, his favorite and most strongly marked historical character, whose career he follows through three different plays, should be nothing more, in disposition, manner, and conversation, than a delineation of his own?

Holinshed, Shakespeare's great authority, from whom he derives the main events in Prince Henry's career, thus describes the Prince: "Indeed, he was youthfully given, grown to audacity; and had chosen him companions, with whom he spent the time in such recreations and delights as he fancied. Yet it would seem, by the report of some writers, that his behavior was not offensive, or at least tending to the damage of anybody; since he had a care to avoid doing of wrong and to tender his affections within the tract of virtue, whereby he opened unto himself a ready passage of good liking among the prudent sort, and was beloved of such as could discern his disposition." And elsewhere the same chronicler says : " This king, even at first appointing with himself to show that princely honors should change public manners, determined to put on him the shape of a new man. For whereas aforetime he had made himself a companion unto misruly mates of dissolute order and life, he now banished them all from his presence ; and in their places chose men of gravity, wit, and high policy, by whose wise counsel he might at all times rule to his honor and dignity." And old Caxton speaks of him as "a noble prince after he was king and crowned ; howbeit, in his youth he had been wild, reckless, and spared nothing of his lusts and desires."

Human nature is the same in prince and peasant ; men and women are all moved by the same passions and desires, no matter what their rank or station ; and Shakespeare saw in this prince a man

with whom he had much in common,
with whose erring youth and misruly
mates he had large sympathy from simi-
larity of experience, and for whose subsequent reformation and heroic career he
had warm and enthusiastic admiration.
The Prince was an Englishman, his
countryman, a man who had shed luster
on the name and history of his country;
a man who lived at a time not so very
remote from his own but that he could
readily transport himself into it; and he
saw in his career and character his own
reflected as in a glass, his youth recalled
as by a wonderful coincidence; and he determined to display it on the stage.   Like
the Prince, he had in his youth been led
into wild and irregular courses ; yet "his
behavior had not been offensive, nor
tending to the damage of anybody," and
doubtless he took care "to avoid doing
of wrong, and to tender his affections
within the tract of virtue, whereby he
would open unto himself a ready passage
of good liking among the prudent sort,
and be beloved of such as could discern

his disposition." He therefore naturally felt drawn toward a man who had undergone the same ordeal as he had, incurred the same obloquy, experienced the same "durance vile" for defiance of authority, and finally emerged unscathed into a nobler and higher sphere of life, shedding luster on his country and glorifying the English name. Undoubtedly it was of himself and his own youth that he thought when he caused the Prince's father to say :

> Most subject is the fattest soil to weeds,
> And he, the noble image of my youth,
> Is overspread with them.

Shakespeare, therefore, was conscious of the fact, that he needed but to draw upon his own life and experience to give a perfect picture of the man whom he resembled ; and it was consequently a labor of love for him

> to tell the world,
> England did never owe so sweet a hope,
> So much misconstrued in his wantonness.

For the Poet was, you may be sure, even

in youth, a prince among his fellows, the first and foremost among the associates of his youth as among those of his manhood.   Let the reader, familiar with Shakespeare, call to mind his impression of the character of Prince Henry, as delineated in the First and the Second Part of *Henry IV.;* let him think of him as he showed himself in his wit-combats with Falstaff; in his thoughtful yet sarcastic encounters with Poins; in his kindly demeanor toward Mrs. Quickly and her "loggerheads"; in his good-natured and fun-loving pranks with the tapster Francis; in his ready appreciation and kindly recognition of Falstaff's witty page; in his noble behavior toward his father and his brothers, and in his generous conduct over the defeated and dying Hotspur;—let him remember the vein of philosophy and deep thinking that runs through all his talk, notwithstanding its looseness, and his eloquent and poetic utterances in his interviews with his father; let him call to mind his familiarity with the common people, with Tom, Dick and Francis, and his ability to "drink with any tinker in his own language during his life"; his love of punning and witticisms, his quips, cranks, and quiddities;—let him recall all these things, and he cannot fail to perceive that this character is such as he and all the world have ever associated with that of the gentle, wise and large-hearted poet Shakespeare. Let him follow me a little farther, and I shall lay before him matter which, without the aid of riddles, ciphers, or mysteries of any kind, must convince him, almost beyond doubt, that the Prince and the Poet are one and the same person.

CHAPTER III.

THE ARGUMENT CONTINUED AND FORTI-
FIED—HOW GENIUS GETS AN EDUCA-
TION.

BEFORE taking up the Prince in the
order in which he appears, and going
right on with him to the end, let me first
complete the impression made by the extract I gave from the opening scene in
Henry V., and thus show how this interesting Prince, full of knowledge and
power, came by his education :

    Arch.   The king is full of grace and fair regard.
    Bish.   And a true lover of the holy Church.
    Arch.   The courses of his youth promised it not.
The breath no sooner left his father's body,
But that his wildness, mortified in him,
Seemed to die too : yea, at that very moment,
Consideration like an angel came,
And whipped the offending Adam out of him,
Leaving his body as a paradise,
To envelop and contain celestial spirits.
Never was such a sudden scholar made :

Never came reformation in a flood,
With such a heady current, scouring faults;
Nor never hydra-headed wilfulness
So soon did lose his seat, and all at once,
As in this king.
   Bish. We are blessed in the change.
   Arch. Hear him but reason in divinity,
And, all-admiring, with an inward wish
You would desire the king were made a prelate:
Hear him debate of commonwealth affairs,
You would say it hath been all-in-all his study:
List his discourse of war, and you shall hear
A fearful battle rendered you in music:
Turn him to any cause of policy,
The Gordian knot of it he will unloose,
Familiar as his garter; that, when he speaks,
The air, a chartered libertine, is still,
And the mute wonder lurketh in men's ears,
To steal his sweet and honey'd sentences;
So that the art and practic part of life
Must be the mistress to his theoric:
Which is a wonder, how his grace should glean it,
Since his addiction was to courses vain;
His companions unlettered, rude, and shallow;
His hours filled up with riots, banquets, sports;
And never noted in him any study,
Any retirement, any sequestration
From open haunts and popularity.

This is precisely the language of those
who now say Shakespeare could not have

2

been the author of the works attributed to him, and seems by a kind of prophecy to have been made to answer them. Now mark how the Bishop is made to explain how such a man may come by his knowledge :

Bish. The strawberry grows underneath the nettle,
And wholesome berries thrive and ripen best
Neighbored by fruit of baser quality :
And so the prince obscured his contemplation
Under the veil of wildness ; which, no doubt,
Grew like the summer grass, fastest by night,
Unseen, yet crescive in his faculty.
Arch. It must be so ; for miracles are ceased,
And therefore we must needs admit the means
How things are perfected.

How significant, how autobiographical these lines seem, in the light of what we know of Shakespeare ! Is it not plain that a man may study, grow, ripen, and become wise and capable without all the world knowing the process ? Is it not evident that his power and knowledge may grow,

Like the summer grass, fastest by night,
Unseen, yet crescive in his faculty ?

Shakespeare undoubtedly studied when most people thought he was asleep. His early years in Stratford—where he is supposed to have written *Venus and Adonis*—were, we may be sure, by no means studyless years; for a man of genius *will* study ; it is the breath of his nostrils ; no man of genius was ever known not to study. Study, or as the Archbishop puts it, contemplation is the very life, the very food of his soul ; and he cannot exist without it. So that he probably owed much more to midnight oil than anybody ever suspected. Miracles have indeed ceased, and therefore we must admit that men attain perfection by other means than by the direct interposition of Providence. How many minds there are that, by self-exertion alone, have equalled those most carefully trained by pedagogues and professors ! These are they that, "crescive in their faculty, grow like the summer grass, fastest by night," in quiet and silent meditation ; these are they that have made, not merely books, but the world the subject of their studies ; not merely science, but men and women, institutions, governments, and passing events ; and the result is a large and liberal intellectual culture, without pedantry or self-conceit, and with faculties working free of all narrow rules and regulations.

The chief argument of the believers in the Baconian theory is, that while Shakespeare was a man of little or no literary culture, and had passed his youth in common labor,

> His companies unlettered, rude, and shallow ;
> His hours filled up with riots, banquets, sports ;
> And never noted in him any study,
> Any retirement, any sequestration
> From open haunts and popularity,

Bacon was from his earliest years the child of culture, the recipient of the best training of his day, the companion of princes, statesmen, scholars, and refined people, and a thinker and student all his life ; and that none but a man of this stamp could have composed the plays which go under Shakespeare's name. Lord Bacon was all they claim him to be, a man of wonderful powers and vast learning; but those who advance this argument against Shakespeare know nothing of the nature and working of genius. Such people seem to be unaware of the fact, that some of the finest minds the world ever saw grew to maturity and worked most of their wonders without having received any special training, without being endowed with any extraordinary culture, and without having had the advantage of any society beyond the commonest; and that some of the finest productions, in art and literature, that the world possesses, are the work of men who spent their lives amid rude and unlettered companions. Bunyan, who wrote the finest allegory produced in 2000 years, and whose style as a writer is unsurpassed for force, beauty, and simplicity, was a common tinker, whose associates were tinkers, tapsters, bell-ringers, soldiers, and puritanical ranters, and who had learned little more than to read the English Bible; Burns, the first and finest poet of Scotland, whose works are read and admired by the whole civilized world, was a common laboring peasant, up to his knees in dirt and manure till his twenty-eighth year, with hardly any schooling to speak of, and with none but cattle, carters, and country bumpkins for companions ; Lincoln, the first and foremost of American statesmen, whose speeches in the campaign against Douglas and whose address at Gettysburg will stand comparison with the best utterances of our most polished orators, was born in a log-cabin in the wild West and bred as a common rail-splitter and boatman.   What education these men had, they got, like every man of real power, by self-exertion, by their own quiet, unaided efforts.   No man, not even the college-graduate, acquires through the teaching of others the power which makes him what he is ; no man ever acquires any real mental power except by his own efforts ; and no man ever attained distinction in art or literature except by what he taught himself.   It is only when the scholar has broken away from his teachers and begun to teach himself that he commences to gain power; it is only when his mind begins to work of its own accord that it commences to expand into independent activity. Not scholastic nor literary lore; not intellectual training nor foreign travel; not the companionship of princes nor of refined and cultured people; none of these things supplies the Promethean spark which enables the poet to work his wonders;— it is something finer, nobler, rarer than any or all of these things; it is that divine essence which we call genius, that intellectual light which comes from God through nature, which shines steadily or fitfully in the peasant as in the prince, and which all other things may aid, but which none can create.

Let me give one or two more examples. Here is our most famous and perhaps most highly admired American orator, Patrick Henry, who spent nearly all his time, till his fortieth year, in fishing and hunting in the rivers and woods of Virginia, becoming familiar with nature

and man in their wildest state, and car-
ing almost as little for books as the abo-
rigines with whom he associated.   He
was literally a denizen of the woods most
of his life, and never took a book in hand
except when compelled to do so.   It was
in this free and independent way of living that he acquired that passionate love
of liberty for which he was afterwards
distinguished, and which he so eloquently
expressed in his famous speech against
George III.   He had been at one time
a store-keeper, at another, according to
Jefferson, a bar-keeper, at another a student at law ; and when he presented himself before the examiners to secure his
license to practice, he was found to be so
deficient in legal knowledge that it was
only by special favor that he obtained
his license; and yet, when the Revolu-
tionary war broke out, and duty sum-
moned him to action, he suddenly burst
upon the world as an orator of the first
rank, a man of remarkable power, whose
speeches annihilated all opposition and
determined the fate of the nation in a

great crisis; a man who stood head and shoulders above all the learned and college-bred men by whom he was surrounded.

Here is Charles James Fox, one of the ablest of English statesmen and most eloquent of English orators, of whom Sir Philip Francis, who knew him well, made this remarkable statement: "They know nothing of Mr. Fox who think that he was what is commonly called *well educated.* I know that he was directly or very nearly the reverse. His mind educated itself; not by early study or instruction, but by active listening and rapid apprehension. He said so himself in the House of Commons when he and Mr. Burke parted—[that he had learned more from the conversation of Mr. Burke than from all the books he had ever read]. His powerful understanding grew like a forest oak, not by cultivation, but by neglect."

"Grew by neglect!" what an expression! It seems to hit the mark exactly, not only with regard to the great orator,

but with regard to the great dramatist.
For if the mind of the English statesman
and orator could grow by neglect, why
not that of his great countryman, the all-
observing and all-absorbing Shakespeare?
Who does not know that there are certain plants which flourish best when free
from all restraint? and who has not heard
of men and women who declared they
prospered best when entirely free from
the restraints and restrictions of the pedagogue and the ferule? "His powerful
understanding grew like a forèst oak, not
by cultivation, but by neglect." I thank
thee, Sir Philip, for that word; it is an
inspiration of genius, revealing the true
nature of genius: it is Junius describing Fox. Probably no words could better characterize Shakespeare's education,
which, poor as it may seem to the Baconians, was far better for him than having his head stuffed with Greek parti-
cles and Latin roots. Classical training
might have spoiled him, as it has spoiled
many a man before and since: it might
have squeezed nature out of him, and

moulded him into one of those stiff, formal, pedantic writers of classical poetry that were so common in his day and are not unknown in ours. As it was, he painted English men and manners in English words and in English ways ; he represented his countrymen in the language and in the manner of his countrymen ; he spoke like the common people and thought like the most cultured, and had he received a Greek and Latin training, he might have given all his thoughts a Greek and Latin tinge, and written no better than the rest of the learned dramatic tribe.

Here is the French Shakespeare, Molière, the man who, of all French writers, has most truly observed and painted human nature—this man was brought up to his father's trade, that of a *fripier*, or mender of old clothes. Like Burns's mother, he could

"Gar auld claes look amaist as weel's the new;"

and doubtless his early training served him in good stead in his later occupation as playwright and stage-manager.

It was not until one eventful night in
his fifteenth year, when a kinsman brought
him to see a comedy acted at the Hôtel
de Bourgogne, that he conceived a desire for "something better than he had
known," something fitter for him than
mending and refashioning old clothes;
and a burning thirst for knowledge took
possession of him.   He longed for an
opportunity to cultivate his mind, to
"unroll the ample page of knowledge,
rich with the spoils of time"; and he
succeeded, much against the will of his
father, in gaining admission to a Jesuit
college.   But it is well known that a man
who is thus suddenly awakened to the
importance and beauty of knowledge,
and starving for the want of it, will get
an education in spite of poverty or riches,
danger or difficulty, in spite of the arbitrary rules of pedants, or the dull formal-
ism of professors; and nobody imagines
that Molière became what he was through
the training of schoolmasters.   'Tis true,
O worshipper of Greek-and-Latin culture! this man Molière, the greatest of

all French writers, did learn to clean, mend, and alter old clothes, as a means of earning his bread! Although Shakespeare was the son of a wool-comber, and is said to have worked at his father's trade, he suffered no humiliation thereby, any more than Molière, nor rendered himself less capable of intellectual exertion. A certain amount of manual labor is, in fact, favorable to intellectual exertion. What an honor and what an encouragement to the hardy sons of Toil, to think that the two greatest dramatic poets of the two greatest European nations should belong to their guild!

The great power of genius, the great achievements of genius, come, not from the study of books, but from personal observation and silent reflection. There are many men of eminence who have openly declared, that their college training was worse than useless; that it was nothing but a hindrance to their mental development (for there are very few real teachers in the world); that they had to unlearn most of what they had learned at

college ; and that their real training began
only after leaving college.   It was intercourse with the world that did for them
what their teachers were unable to do :
it was personal experience among men
that awoke in them a thirst for knowledge
and a determination to study for themselves.   " I learned nothing at college,"
says Voltaire, " but Latin and nonsense."
" I am sorry that I ever was sent to college," says Ralph Bernal Osborne, the brilliant parliamentary orator, " for I learned
nothing there but vices and bad habits."
" It is good to go through college," says
Emerson, " to see how little there is in
it ;" and Hazlitt boldly maintains that
"any man who has passed through the
regular gradations of a classical education, and is not made a fool by it, may
consider himself as having had a narrow
escape."

The study of the classics is by no
means always the best thing for a youth
of genius.   Where a dozen young men
come together to discuss questions of
the hour, to talk, to compare views, to

examine systems, or to criticise and laugh at men and things,—that is sometimes the best college for such a youth. Such was Burns's college at Dunfermline ; such was Curran's college at the London debating club ; and such has been the college of many another, who attained distinction without ever setting foot within college walls. It makes no matter how a man gets an education, provided he gets it ; and some get it out of school much better than in it. Half the men who lead public opinion in the United States to-day, as editors and writers, are graduates of a printing-office. "In youth," says Walter Bagehot, "the real plastic energy is not in tutors, or lectures, or in books 'got up' ; but in Homer and Plutarch ; in the books that all read because all like ; in what all talk of because all are interested ; or in the argumentative walk and disputatious lounge ; in the impact of young thought upon young thought, of fresh thought on fresh thought ; of hot thought on hot thought; in mirth and refutation, in ridicule and laughter; for these are the free play of the natural mind;" and these form the most mind-quickening and thought-stirring exercises that the student can engage in. That is why the teacher who instructs without book, who employs his own language instead of that of the book, is so much more successful than the regular word-cramming pedagogue.

In Shakespeare's time, the world was alive with discussion; the human mind, after a sleep of nearly a thousand years, had awakened to a love of knowledge, and had begun in earnest to discuss philosophy, religion, politics, and natural science. Printing, the Reformation, and the discoveries in America and India had set men a-thinking and whetted their appetite for knowledge; and wherever two or three were gathered together, there was a school of thought; there was a college and a training-school for genius. This was the living school in which Shakespeare was educated; this was the school in which his mind expanded into a recognition of its own powers, and in which he began making those observations which he subsequently turned to so good account. Probably he, too, like Fox, learned more from conversation than he did from books. Of one thing we may be sure, that of nothing was he more fond than of talking with men and women who could thus communicate their thoughts, pleasantly or forcibly, one to another.

I have heard Edward Everett Hale say that the best men of Elizabeth's time were taught "to read, write, speak the truth, and hate the Spaniard," and that was all! Yet what mighty men there were in those days! They were indeed giants, giants greater than any in ancient fable or modern romance; and their power came not so much from the study of books, as from actual observation of men and things, from practical thinking and talking on the questions

3

of the day. Like the Duke in *As You Like It*, they could

Find tongues in trees, books in the running brooks,
Sermons in stones, and good in everything.

CHAPTER IV.

THE PRINCE AND THE POET COMPARED.

LET us now go back, and take up the Prince, from the moment in which he is first mentioned by Shakespeare, and go forward with him until that in which he quits the scene of action. We shall find that his character is uniformly that of the Poet ; that it uniformly agrees with all that we know of the Poet ; and that in this play there is a revelation of him beyond that which will be found in any other of his plays. I have said that Shakespeare makes him a chief character in three plays; he forms, in fact, one of the characters in four ; although in one, that in which he is first mentioned, he does not come on the stage. In *Richard III.*, Act V., Scene III., the following passage occurs :

Windsor: A Room in the Court Castle.

Enter BOLINGBROKE *as King;* PERCY, *and other Lords.*

Bol. Can no man tell me of my unthrifty son?
'Tis full three months since I did see him last:
If any plague hang over us, 'tis he.
I would to God, my lords, he might be found.
Inquire at London, 'mongst the taverns there,
For there, they say, he daily doth frequent,
With unrestrained loose companions;
Even such, they say, 'as stand in narrow lanes,
And beat our watch, and rob our passengers;
While he, young wanton, and effeminate boy,
Takes on the point of honor to support
So dissolute a crew.
    Per. My lord, some two days since I saw the
        prince,
And told him of these triumphs held at Oxford.
    Bol. And what said the gallant?
    Per. His answer was,—he would unto the stews,
And from the commonest creature pluck a glove,
And wear it as a favor; and with that
He would unhorse the lustiest challenger.
    Bol. As dissolute as desperate: yet, through
        both
I see some sparks of better hope, which elder days
May happily bring forth.

This skilfully prepares the reader for what is coming. Now observe this full-length portrait of the Prince, as he first appears in the opening scenes of the First Part of *Henry IV.:*

SCENE II. London. A Room in the Palace.
Enter Prince HENRY *and* FALSTAFF.

Fal. Now, Hal, what time of day is it, lad ?

Prince. Thou art so fat-witted with drinking of old sack, and unbuttoning thee after supper, and sleeping upon benches after noon, that thou hast forgotten to demand that truly which thou wouldst truly know. What a devil hast thou to do with the time of the day ? unless hours were cups of sack, and minutes capons, and clocks the tongues of bawds, and dials the signs of leaping-houses, and the blessed sun himself a fair hot wench in flame-colored taffata. I see no reason why thou shouldst be so superfluous to demand the time of the day.

Fal. Indeed, you come near me now, Hal ; for we that take purses go by the moon and the seven stars, and not by Phœbus,—he, "that wandering knight so fair." And I pr'ythee, sweet wag, when thou art king,—as, God save thy grace,—majesty, I should say, for grace thou wilt have none,—

Prince. What ! none ?

Fal. No, by my troth ; not so much as wilt serve to be prologue to an egg and butter.

Prince. Well, how then ? Come, roundly, roundly.

Fal. Marry, then, sweet wag, when thou art king, let not us, that are squires of the night's body, be called thieves of the day's beauty : let us be Diana's foresters, gentlemen of the shade, minions of the moon; and let men say, we be men of good government, being governed as the sea is, by our noble and chaste mistress, the moon, under whose countenance we—steal !

Prince. Thou say'st well, and it holds well, too ; for the fortune of us that are the moon's men doth ebb and flow like the sea, being governed, as the sea is, by the moon. As for proof now : A purse of gold most resolutely snatched on Monday night, and most dissolutely spent on Tuesday morning ; got with swearing—Lay by ; and spent with crying —Bring in ; now in as low an ebb as the foot of the ladder, and by and by in as high a flow as the ridge of the gallows.

Fal. By the Lord, thou say'st true, lad. And is not my hostess of the tavern a most sweet wench ?

Prince. As the honey of Hybla, my old lad of the castle. And is not a buff jerkin a most sweet robe of durance ?

Fal. How now, how now, mad wag ? what, in thy quips and thy quiddities ? what a plague have I to do with a buff jerkin ?

Prince. Why, what a pox have I to do with my hostess of the tavern ?

Fal. Well, thou hast called her to a reckoning, many a time and oft.

Prince. Did I ever call for thee to pay thy part ?

Fal. No : I'll give thee thy due ; thou hast paid all there.

Prince. Yea, and elsewhere, so far as my coin would stretch ; and where it would not, I have used my credit.

Fal. Yea, and so used it, that were it not here apparent that thou art heir apparent,—But, I pr'ythee, sweet wag, shall there be gallows standing in England when thou art king ? and resolution thus fobbed, as it is, with the rusty curb of old father antic the law ? Do not thou, when thou art king, hang a thief.

Prince. No : thou shalt.

Fal. Shall I ? O rare ! By the Lord, I'll be a brave judge.

Prince. Thou judgest false already. I mean, thou shalt have the hanging of the thieves, and so become a rare hangman.

Fal. Well, Hal, well ; and in some sort it jumps with my humor, as well as waiting in the court, I can tell you.

Prince. For obtaining of suits ?

Fal. Yea, for obtaining of suits,—whereof the hangman hath no lean wardrobe. 'Sblood, I am as melancholy as a gib-cat, or a lugged bear.

Prince. Or an old lion ; or a lover's lute.

Fal. Yea, or the drone of a Lincolnshire bag-pipe.

Prince. What say'st thou to a hare, or the melancholy of Moor-ditch ?

Fal. Thou hast the most unsavory similes ;

and art, indeed, the most comparative, rascalliest, sweet young prince.—But, Hal, I pr'ythee, trouble me no more with vanity. I would to God, thou and I knew where a commodity of good names were to be bought. An old lord of the Council rated me the other day in the street about you, sir; but I marked him not: and yet he talked very wisely; but I regarded him not: and yet he talked wisely, and in the street too.

Prince. Thou didst well; for wisdom cries out in the streets, and no man regards it.

Fal. O! thou hast damnable iteration, and art, indeed, able to corrupt a saint. Thou hast done much harm upon me, Hal. God forgive thee for it! Before I knew thee, Hal, I knew nothing; and now am I, if a man should speak truly, little better than one of the wicked. I must give over this life, and I will give it over: by the Lord, an I do not, I am a villain. I'll be damned for never a king's son in Christendom.

Prince. Where shall we take a purse to-morrow, Jack?

Fal. Zounds! where thou wilt, lad; I'll make one; an I do not, call me villain, and baffle me.

Prince. I see a good amendment of life in thee: from praying to purse-taking.

Enter POINS, *at a distance.*

Fal. Why, Hal, 'tis my vocation, Hal [*i. e. a plunder-seeking soldier*]: 'Tis no sin for a man to labor in his vocation. Poins!—Now shall we know if Gadshill have set a match. O! if men were to be saved by merit, what hole in hell were hot enough for him! This is the most omnipotent villain that ever cried, Stand! to a true man.

Prince. Good morrow, Ned.

Poins. Good morrow, sweet Hal.—What says Monsieur Remorse? What says Sir John Sack-and-Sugar? Jack, how agrees the devil and thee about thy soul, that thou soldest him, on Good-Friday last, for a cup of Madeira and a cold capon's leg?

Prince. Sir John stands to his word; the devil shall have his bargain; for he was never yet a breaker of proverbs: he will give the devil his due.

Poins. Then art thou damned for keeping thy word with the devil.

Prince. Else he had been damned for cozening the devil.

Poins. But, my lads, my lads, to-morrow morning by four o'clock, early at Gadshill. There are pilgrims going to Canterbury with rich offerings, and traders riding to London with fat purses. I have visors for you all; you have horses for yourselves. Gadshill lies to-night in Rochester; I have bespoke supper to-morrow night in Eastcheap: we may do it as secure as sleep. If you will go, I will stuff your purses full of crowns; if you will not, tarry at home and be hanged.

Fal. Hear ye, Yedward: if I tarry at home, and go not, I'll hang you for going.

Poins. You will, chops?

Fal. Hal, wilt thou make one?

Prince. Who, I rob? I a thief? Not I, by my faith.

Fal. There's neither honesty, manhood, nor good fellowship in thee, nor thou cam'st not of the blood royal, if thou dar'st not stand for ten shillings [the *royal* or *real* was a coin worth ten shillings].

Prince. Well, then, once in my life I'll be a madcap.

Fal. Why, that's well said.

Prince. Well, come what will, I'll tarry at home.

Fal. By the Lord, I'll be a traitor, then, when thou art king.

Prince. I care not.

Poins. Sir John, I pr'ythee, leave the prince and me alone: I will lay him down such reasons for this adventure, that he shall go.

Fal. Well, God give thee the spirit of persuasion, and him the ears of profiting, that what thou speakest may move, and what he hears may be believed, that the true prince may (for recreation's sake) prove a false thief; for the poor abuses of the time want countenance. Farewell: You shall find me in Eastcheap.

Prince. Farewell, thou latter spring! Farewell, All-hallown summer!   [*Exit* FALSTAFF.

Poins. Now, my good, sweet, honey lord, ride with us to-morrow. I have a jest to execute that I cannot manage alone. Falstaff, Bardolph, Peto and Gadshill, shall rob those men that we have already waylaid: yourself and I will not be there;

and when they have the booty, if you and I do not rob them, cut this head from my shoulders.

Prince. How shall we part with them in setting forth ?

Poins. Why, we will set forth before or after them, and appoint them a place of meeting, wherein it is at our pleasure to fail; and then will they adventure upon the exploit themselves, which they shall have no sooner achieved, but we'll set upon them.

Prince. Ay, but 'tis like that they will know us by our horses, by our habits, and by every other appointment, to be ourselves.

Poins. Tut! our horses they shall not see; I'll tie them in the wood: our visors we will change, after we leave them; and, sirrah, I have cases of buckram for the nonce, to inmask our noted outward garments.

Prince. Yea, but I doubt they will be too hard for us.

Poins. Well, for two of them, I know them to be as true-bred cowards as ever turned back; and for the third, if he fight longer than he sees reason, I'll forswear arms. The virtue of this jest will be the incomparable lies that this same fat rogue will tell us when we meet at supper: how thirty, at least, he fought with; what wards, what blows, what extremities he endured; and, in the reproof of this, lies the jest.

Prince. Well, I'll go with thee. Provide us all

things necessary, and meet me to-morrow night in
Eastcheap ; there I'll sup.   Farewell.

Poins.   Farewell, my lord.   [*Exit* POINS.

Prince.   I know you all, and will a while uphold
The unyoked humor of your idleness :
Yet herein will I imitate the sun,
Who doth permit the base contagious clouds
To smother up his beauty from the world,
That, when he please again to be himself,
Being wanted, he may be more wondered at,
By breaking through the foul and ugly mists
Of vapors, that did seem to strangle him.
If all the year were playing holidays,
To sport would be as tedious as to work ;
But, when they seldom come, they wished-for come,
And nothing pleaseth but rare accidents.
So, when this loose behavior I throw off,
And pay the debt I never promised,
By how much better than my word I am,
By so much shall I falsify men's hopes ;
And, like bright metal on a sullen ground,
My reformation, glittering o'er my fault,
Shall show more goodly, and attract more eyes,
Than that which hath no foil to set it off.
I'll so offend, to make offence a skill,
Redeeming time when men think least I will.

Talk about the wit-combats between
Shakespeare and Ben Jonson !   Talk
about the loss to literature from want of a

Boswell to report them !   Why, here they are, reported by Shakespeare himself! What finer specimens of such combats could be had than these?   These are Shakespeare's wit-combats with the wittiest man he knew ; these are specimens of his talks with his fellows ; these are the scenes which he drew from his own life and experience.   Who does not feel that these are the words "so nimble and so full of subtle flame," which, after their author's departure from the Mermaid Tavern, "left an air behind them which alone was able to make the next two companies right witty?"   Shakespeare, who "never blotted a line," wrote as easily as he talked, and talked as wittily and wisely as he wrote.   He was, like the Prince, a lover of good things of all kinds; of good books, good conversation, good wine, good company.   That the Prince was well acquainted with general literature, is evident ; that he was familiar with the Bible is equally so, and that, notwithstanding the levity of many of his speeches, he thought deeply on life and

death, and observed carefully the characters of men, is perfectly clear. He was,
in fact, notwithstanding his wildness, one
of the most accomplished princes of his
time, and we shall see that the Poet
makes him resemble his creator in this
respect.

I beg the reader to notice carefully
this last speech of the Prince, for it throws
a flood of light on his character, and, to
my mind, connects it unmistakably with
that of the Poet. Let him observe the
wise reflection, the cool, philosophic contemplation, behind " the veil of wildness,"
which it displays. Let him notice that it
shows plainly he is not *one of them*, but
an observer, a player among them, whose
objects are far different from theirs. For
what does this line mean,

I'll so offend, to make offence a skill,

but this : " My whole desperate conduct
is nothing more than a piece of skilful
acting, to make my real character shine
all the brighter by-and-by ?" And who
does not know that there have been oth-

ers, quite as philosophic, quite as gifted as he, who also sought "rare accidents" to relieve the tedium of the time? Who, that is acquainted with the life of Lord Byron, for instance, does not know that he played a part and made himself "a motley to the view," from sheer eccentricity of genius?

But still more significant is this line:

Redeeming time when men think least I will.

What a world of meaning there is in that line! Is not this another evidence that he studied when nobody knew of it? This is the key, the secret of his success; the explanation of his wonderful knowledge, his vast acquaintance with history, literature, science and art. Who has not seen the same thing exemplified in the lives of other eminent and successful men? This is how most men of eminence gain their knowledge; this is how genius works; how it acquires an education and accomplishes its wonders. The Poet was silently working and laying in stores of knowledge and wisdom when the rest of mankind were snoring; laying in stores of knowledge at a time when men thought least he would. This, therefore, is plainly a leaf from his own experience. "It is certain," says that admirable Shakespearean scholar, Mr. Hudson, "that in mental and literary accomplishment the Prince was far in advance of the age, being in fact as well one of the most finished gentlemen as of the greatest statesmen and best men of his time. It was for the old chroniclers to talk of his miraculous conversion. Shakespeare, in a far wiser spirit, brings his conduct within the ordinary rules and measures of human character, representing whatsoever changes occur in him as proceeding by the methods and proportions of nature." Precisely; his own nature and experience. He had been such a man; he had done such things; and he had doubtless acted with similar motives.

Notice how conscious the Prince is, even while associating with evil-doers, and apparently furthering their wicked devices, of the consequences of evil deeds. No sooner has he described the ebb and flow of the purse of the thief, than he adds, " Now in as low an ebb as the foot of the ladder, and by-and-by in as high a flow as the ridge of the gallows !" And when Falstaff asks, immediately after, " Is not my hostess of the tavern a most sweet wench ? " the Prince replies : " As the honey of Hybla, my old lad of the castle. And is not a buff jerkin [*the coat of a sheriff's officer*] a most sweet robe of durance?" That is: "Oh yes, she is very amiable ; but is it not a sweet thing to go to prison, by running in debt to this wench ? "

Thus we see that, in the Prince's mind, the consequences of evil-doing are always present, and he toys with evil and evil-doers without actually becoming one of them. Toys, did I say? Nay, not so ; he thus plainly intimates to Falstaff that evil-doing leads to the most dire and disgraceful consequences ; which agrees perfectly with the conduct of the Poet himself ; for we find that he avoided the

4

disgraceful deeds and wretched dissipation of most of the other dramatists of
his time.   Let any one who knows something of the lives of Marlowe, Greene,
Peele, and the rest, as well as of the life
of the Poet, compare their wild and reckless careers with that of the wise, prudent and gentle Shakespeare—his thrift
in his profession, his care to live on an
independent footing, his noble friends
and associates, his kindness to Ben Jonson, his generosity toward his father—
and then say if he did not, like the
Prince, and unlike them, have a horror of
the " buff jerkin " and the "most sweet
robe of durance!"

CHAPTER V.

ANOTHER VIEW OF THE POET IN THE PRINCE.

THE Prince next appears in the Gadshill robbery scene, and after Falstaff and the rest attack and despoil the travellers, he and Poins attack and despoil the thieves, and in high good humor speed away for London.

> *Prince.* Got with much ease. Now merrily to
>   horse :
> The thieves are scattered, and possessed with fear
> So strongly, that they dare not meet each other ;
> Each takes his fellow for an officer.
> Away, good Ned ! Falstaff sweats to death,
> And lards the lean earth as he walks along :
> Wer't not for laughing, I should pity him.
> *Poins.*   How the rogue roared !

Now comes a scene which is more characteristic of Shakespeare than almost anything in the play. It is the scene between the Prince and Francis the pot-

boy, just before the re-entrance of Falstaff
with his hacked sword and blood-stained
garments.   One word before presenting
this scene.   The patience and gentle indulgence which Shakespeare showed to
the common people of his acquaintance
is proved by the fact that he was loved
by all who knew him.   He listened with
patience and interest to the talk of the
poorest parrot of a man, and took care
not to hurt him.   "He was too wise not
to know," says Walter Bagehot, "that
for most of the purposes of human life,
stupidity is a most valuable element.
He had nothing of the impatience which
sharp, logical, narrow minds habitually
feel when they come across those who
do not apprehend their quick and pre-
cise deductions.   No doubt he talked
to the stupid players, to the stupid door-
keeper, to the property man, who con-
siders paste jewels 'very preferable, besides the expense,'—talked with the stupid apprentices of stupid Fleet Street,
and had much pleasure in ascertaining
what was their notion of *King Lear*."

Now, bearing this in mind, and recollecting his delightful and loving delineation of that prince of blockheads, Dogberry, let the reader peruse carefully the following scene, and say if the Prince is not Shakespeare himself. Let him especially observe his statement at the opening, that he had been "with three or four loggerheads, had sounded the very base string of humility, and could call them all by their Christian names." Let him recollect that the Boar's-Head Tavern was very near the Blackfriar's Play-house, and that it was in fact a known resort of Shakespeare and his companions.

Eastcheap.   A Room in the Boar's-Head Tavern.

Enter Prince HENRY *and* POINS.

Prince.   Ned, pr'ythee, come out of that fat room and lend me thy hand to laugh a little.

Poins.   Where hast been, Hal?

Prince.   With three or four loggerheads, amongst three or four-score hogsheads.   I have sounded the very base string of humility.   Sirrah, I am sworn brother to a leash of drawers, and can call them all by their Christian names, as—Tom, Dick and Francis.   They take it already upon their salvation, that though I be but prince of Wales, yet I am the king of courtesy, and tell me flatly I am no proud Jack, like Falstaff, but a Corinthian, a lad of mettle, a good boy (by the Lord so they call me); and when I am king of England, I shall command all the good lads of Eastcheap. They call drinking deep, dying scarlet; and when you breathe in your watering, they cry hem! and bid you play it off.—To conclude, I am so good a proficient in one quarter of an hour, that I can drink with any tinker in his own language during my life. I tell thee, Ned, thou hast lost much honor that thou wert not with me in this action. But, sweet Ned,—to sweeten which name of Ned, I give thee this pennyworth of sugar, clapped even now in my hand by an under-skinker [*tapster*]; one that never spake other English in his life than—"Eight shillings and sixpence," and—"You are welcome;" with this shrill addition —"Anon, anon, sir! Score a pint of bastard in the Half-moon," or so. But, Ned, to drive away the time till Falstaff come, I pr'ythee, do thou stand in some by-room, while I question my puny drawer to what end he gave me the sugar; and do thou never leave calling—Francis! that his tale to me may be nothing but—Anon! Step aside, and I'll show thee a precedent.

Poins. Francis!

Prince. Thou art perfect.

Poins. Francis!   [*Exit* POINS.

Enter FRANCIS.

Fran. Anon, anon, sir. Look down into the Pomegranate, Ralph.

Prince. Come hither, Francis.

Fran. My lord.

Prince. How long hast thou to serve, Francis?

Fran. Forsooth, five year, and as much as to—

Poins. [*Within.*] Francis!

Fran. Anon, anon, sir.

Prince. Five years! by'r lady, a long lease for the clinking of pewter. But, Francis, darest thou be so valiant as to play the coward with thy indenture, and to show it a fair pair of heels, and run from it?

Fran. O Lord, sir! I'll be sworn upon all the books in England, I could find in my heart—

Poins. [*Within.*] Francis!

Fran. Anon, anon, sir.

Prince. How old art thou, Francis?

Fran. Let me see,—about Michaelmas next I shall be—

Poins. [*Within.*] Francis!

Fran. Anon, sir.—Pray you, stay a little, my lord.

Prince. Nay, but hark you, Francis. For the sugar thou gavest me,—'twas a pennyworth, was't not?

Fran. O Lord, sir, I would it had been two.

Prince. I will give thee for it a thousand pound: ask me when thou wilt, and thou shalt have it.

Poins. [*Within.*] Francis!

Fran. Anon, anon.

Prince. Anon, Francis? No, Francis; but to-

morrow, Francis; or, Francis, on Thursday; or, indeed, Francis, when thou wilt. But, Francis,—

Fran. My lord?

Prince. Wilt thou rob this leathern-jerkin,
crystal-button, nott-pated, agate-ring, puke-stock-
ing, caddis-garter, smooth-tongue, Spanish pouch,—

Fran. O Lord, sir! who do you mean?

Prince. Why, then, your brown bastard is your
only drink; for, look you, your white canvas doub-
let will sully. In Barbary, sir, it cannot come to so
much.

Fran. What, sir?

Poins. [*Within.*] Francis!

Prince. Away, you rogue! Dost not thou hear
them call?

[*Here they both call him; the drawer stands amazed,
not knowing which way to go.*

Enter VINTNER.

Vint. What! standest thou still, and hear'st such
a calling? Look to the guests within. [*Exit* FRAN.]
My lord, old Sir John, with half a dozen more, are at
the door; shall I let them in?

Prince. Let them alone awhile, and then open
the door. [*Exit* VINTNER.] Poins!

Re-enter POINS.

Poins. Anon, anon, sir.

Prince. Sirrah, Falstaff and the rest of the
thieves are at the door; shall we be merry?

Poins. As merry as crickets, my lad. But hark
ye: what cunning match have you made with this
jest of the drawer? Come, what's the issue?

Prince. I am now of all humors, that have showed themselves humors, since the old days of goodman Adam, to the pupil age of this twelve o'clock at midnight.

Re-enter FRANCIS *with wine.*

What's o'clock, Francis?

Fran. Anon, anon, sir.   [*Exit.*

Prince. That ever this fellow should have fewer words than a parrot, and yet the son of a woman. His industry is—up-stairs, and down-stairs ; his eloquence, the parcel of a reckoning. I am not yet of Percy's mind, the Hotspur of the North ; he that kills me some six or seven dozen Scots at a breakfast, washes his hands, and says to his wife,—" Fie upon this quiet life ! I want work." " O my sweet Harry," says she, " how many hast thou killed to-day ? " " Give my roan horse a drench," says he ; and answers, " Some fourteen," an hour after ; " a trifle, a trifle." I pr'ythee, call in Falstaff. I'll play Percy, and that damned brawn shall play Dame Mortimer, his wife. " Rivo ! " says the drunkard. Call in ribs, call in tallow.

I should not be surprised if the Poet and one of his professional chums had, on some occasion, played this very trick on the drawer of the Blackfriar's or the Boar's-Head Tavern. Nothing is more likely. It looks, for all the world, like one of the practical jokes which he and

Burbage are said to have played together; such as have often since been played
by Brougham, by Sothern and by other
dramatic celebrities of our time.

This point of familiarity with the people, of kindly and appreciative association with the humblest sort of people,
is a prime characteristic of Shakespeare.
What a marvellous revelation of this trait
is shown, in making the Prince become
so familiar with a tapster as to allow him
to present him with a lump of sugar! Is
not this Shakespeare? Is not this the
man who knew all classes of men so intimately? Mr. Walter Bagehot, in his
excellent Essay on "Shakespeare, the
Man," has some very wise remarks on
this head. After showing the striking
resemblance between Shakespeare and
Scott in their love of the common people, and the equally striking dissimilar-
ity, in this respect, of Goethe to both of
them, he says: "If you will describe the
people, nay, if you will write for the people, you must be one of the people.
You must have led their life, and must

wish to lead their life. . . . . . Any attempt to produce a likeness of what is not really *liked* by the person who is attempting it, will end in the creation of what may be correct, but is not living— of what may be artistic, but is likewise artificial." Was it not thus that Shakespeare succeeded in portraying men so well? He *liked* the people, and could associate familiarly with the commonest among them.

Consider for a moment the dramatic presentation of Egmont and Clärchen as compared with that of Brutus and Portia, or of Hotspur and Lady Percy. The popular hero, the successful general, the idol of a nation, high-spirited Egmont, is travestied by Goethe into something marvellously like himself, a heartless deceiver of young women! With him the people were mere ciphers to work out literary or scientific problems; the means of ministering to the desires and the pleasures of the rich and gifted; and while his countrymen were engaged in a death-struggle for their very existence as a people, he could amuse himself by making chemical experiments on their bones in the graveyards!

Scott, who was fond of associating familiarly with the common people, and noting their ways and thoughts, was heartily loved by them; and we know that Shakespeare was loved by all who knew him. One of Scott's striking remarks is, that he "had heard higher sentiments from his poor uneducated neighbors than he had ever met with outside of the pages of the Bible." He knew how to make the poor and humble feel at home with him, how to make them show their inner selves; and he knew how to reproduce their rude but significant ways of expressing their thoughts. He had always a smile, a kind word, and a pinch of snuff for every laboring man of his acquaintance whom he met, and chatted with him as pleasantly as if he were his friend. When he visited one of his titled friends, he was likely to become as familiar with the coachman of his host as with the host himself; and there was not a dog in the household on whom he did not cast a smile of kindly interest. In his own country, he was so much loved by the people, that there was not a house on the Border in which he was not heartily welcome. "Sir Walter speaks to every man as if he were his blood relation," was the expressive remark of one of his dependants.

Goethe, on the other hand, kept aloof from the people; he was not one of them, and never wanted to be; he was essentially an aristocrat in feeling, and had little sympathy for the ways and habits of the common people; consequently, neither his language nor his thoughts are theirs; in fact, he wrote in a language which the common people of his day no more understood than if it were Greek, and which is Greek to some of the most intelligent among them to-day. He was, in truth, essentially Greek in his nature and culture; a lover of beauty of the ideal, æsthetic sort; a student of pure science for the sake of truth alone; not a lover of mankind as they are; and he is accordingly read and appreciated by studied people, by scholars and the university-bred generally; who, it must be remembered, are by no means the best judges of literature. Scott, like Shakespeare, abounds in characters drawn from the common people, characters whom he loved, real living characters, who are known, remembered, and cherished by all who make their acquaintance. Goethe has not one such character, and neither he nor any character he created is loved by the people. So that, having no sympathy with the common people, they have none with him, and care nothing for him or his books.

Shakespeare not only associated familiarly with the common people, and noted with interest their habits, their ways, and their thoughts, but having sprung from them himself, he always found himself at home among them. And when he became a writer for the stage, he obviously kept up his familiar relations with them; he so demeaned himself as to make them feel at home with him, and thus enjoyed the full flavor of their life and conversation. Now this is precisely the conduct of the Prince. He puts himself on a level with the lowest of the people, calls them familiarly Tom, Dick, and Francis, and is so loved by them that they will fight to the death for him. They " tell him flatly he is no proud Jack like Falstaff," and that " when he is king of England he shall command all the good lads in Eastcheap." One of them, a poor tapster, even comes and gives him a piece of sugar by way of a present! Could any great man be more tenderly loved by the common people than this? To make a Prince become "sworn brother to a leash of drawers," and such a proficient in the language of the vulgar as to be able to "drink with any tinker in his own language," would, in the hands of any other writer, probably turn out a shocking and degrading spectacle ; but in Shakespeare's hands it is quite natural, because it is just what Shakespeare did himself, and which he found in no way degrading.   There was hardly any sphere of life with which he was not acquainted, and probably few with which his acquaintance was not personal.   So that he could not only "drink with any tinker in his own language," but associate with the noblest man in England on his own footing, and outdo him in nobility of behavior, language, and thought.   Indeed, Davies, who probably knew him personally, has, in his "Scourge of Folly," published in 1611, this excellent epigram on him :

Some say, good Will, which I in sport do sing,
  Hadst thou not played some kingly parts in sport,
Thou hadst been a companion for a king,
  And been a king among the meaner sort.

He seems to have been especially fond of a genial, witty, and open-hearted companion.   He was doubtless as fond of Falstaff as Falstaff was of him ; for he preferred laughter to tears, and probably no man enjoyed a good joke better than he.   " In no point does Shakespeare ex·

aggerate," says Carlyle, "but only in laughter. His laughter seems to pour from him in floods." This is the charm that the Prince finds in Falstaff: this is the spell by which he holds him: he could make him "laugh till his face was like a wet cloak ill laid up!" "When a man has created such a character as Falstaff," says Bagehot, "without a capacity for laughter, then a blind man may succeed in describing colors. Intense animal spirits are the single sentiment—if they be a sentiment—of the entire character. If most men were to save up all the gayety of their whole lives, it would come to about the gayety of one speech in Falstaff. A morose man might have amassed many jokes, might have observed many details of jovial society, might have conceived a Sir John, marked by rotundity of body; but could hardly have imagined what we call his rotundity of mind."

Thus, then, this point is, I think, pretty clearly made out : that the Prince, loving wit and humor wherever he found

5

them, or curiously observing dulness and stupidity, was fond of mingling familiarly with the people, and talking freely and easily with them ; and in this the Poet simply presented in the Prince a faithful portrait of himself.*

---

* While this work is passing through the press, I have had a glance at Mr. Donnelly's long-promised book, "The Great Cryptogram." Will the reader believe his own eyes, when I tell him, that Mr. Donnelly gravely maintains, that because Falstaff, in the robbery scene, exclaims, "On, *bacons*, on!" and the name *Francis* is, in the scene between the Prince and the pot-boy, repeated twenty times, *Francis Bacon* must have written the plays! Surely this is profundity beyond example. Shakespearean criticism with a vengeance! I think this discovery is about as good as that of the man who said he knew who had written Shakespeare's plays; he had seen the name at the end of the book; his name was "Finis"!

I shall have something to say of this Donnelly business in a subsequent chapter.

CHAPTER VI.

"LOOK HERE UPON THIS PICTURE, AND THEN ON THIS!"

HERE is another conversation between the Prince and Poins, which, if it do not show the former as a man of the people, familiar with the ways and thoughts of the people, loving the common things of the people, even "small beer," and, notwithstanding his rank, enjoying to the full all the common pleasures of the people, then is there no such man in literature. There is something, indeed, so quietly like the man Shakespeare all over this scene, that it mightily fortifies my supposition that the Poet simply drew his own in the character of the Prince :

SCENE II. London : A street.

Enter Prince HENRY *and* POINS.

Prince. Trust me, I am exceeding weary.

Poins. Is it come to that? I had thought weariness durst not have attached one of so high blood.

Prince. 'Faith it does me, though it discolors the complexion of my greatness to acknowledge it. Doth it not show vilely in me to desire small beer?

Poins. Why, a prince should not be so loosely studied, as to remember so weak a composition.

Prince. Belike, then, my appetite was not princely got; for, by my troth, I do now remember the poor creature, small beer. But, indeed, these humble considerations make me out of love with my greatness. What a disgrace it is to me to remember thy name? or to know thy face to-morrow? or to take note how many pair of silk stockings thou hast; namely, these, and those that were thy peach-colored ones? or to bear the inventory of thy shirts: as, one for superfluity, and one other for use?—but *that* the tennis-court keeper knows better than I, for it is a low ebb of linen with thee, when thou keep'st not racket there; as thou hast not done a great while, because the rest of thy low-countries have made a shift to eat up thy holland; and God knows whether those that bawl out the ruins of thy linen shall inherit His kingdom; but the midwives say, the children are not in the fault, whereupon the world increases, and kindreds are mightily strengthened.

Poins. How ill it follows, after you have labored so hard, you should talk so idly!—Tell me, how many good young princes would do so, their fathers being so sick as yours at this time is?

Prince. Shall I tell thee one thing, Poins?

Poins. Yes, faith ; and let it be an excellent good thing.

Prince. It shall serve among wits of no higher breeding than thine.

Poins. Go to; I stand the push of your one thing that you will tell.

Prince. Marry, I tell thee,—it is not meet that I should be sad, now my father is sick ; albeit I could tell to thee (as to one it pleases me, for fault of a better, to call my friend), I could be sad, and sad indeed too.

Poins. Very hardly, upon such a subject.

Prince. By this hand, thou think'st me as far in the devil's book as thou and Falstaff, for obduracy and persistency. Let the end try the man. But I tell thee, my heart bleeds inwardly that my father is so sick ; and keeping such vile company as thou art hath in reason taken from me all ostentation of sorrow.

Poins. The reason?

Prince. What would'st thou think of me if I should weep?

Poins. I would think thee a most princely hypocrite.

Prince. It would be every man's thought; and thou art a blessed fellow to think as every man thinks. Never a man's thought in the world keeps the roadway better than thine : every man would think me a hypocrite indeed. And what accites your most worshipful thought to think so?

Poins. Why, because you have been so lewd, and so much engraffed to Falstaff.

Prince. And to thee.

Poins. By this light, I am well spoken of: I can hear it with my own ears. The worst that they can say of me is, that I am a second brother, and that I am a proper fellow of my hands; and those two things I confess I cannot help.—By the mass, here comes Bardolph.

"Let the end try the man!" That's it: the Prince is, even in the play, no actual rake and debauchee, but a wise, witty, thoughtful man; charmed, it is true, by the wit and humor of the most fascinating of loose companions, and enjoying for a season the mirth, jollity, and high spirits of a riotous company; but not in spirit one of them. He loves what is good in them, but despises their vices. It is plain that his companions mistake him; they think him as bad as themselves; for Poins obviously thinks him so devoid of natural affection as to be capable of joy at the news of his father's death. But he is mistaken; the Prince is quite a different man. He is by no means "so far in the devil's book" as they are ; and he comes out in the sequel, as the original did, unscathed, and all the wiser for his experience among them. If he were an abandoned rake, how could he be made to act and think so wisely when away from them? how could he encounter and conquer that prince of warriors, Hotspur? and if he were not of a generous heart and philosophic mind, how could he be made to pronounce such a noble speech over the dead body of this his conquered enemy?—

             Fare thee well, great heart!—
Ill-weaved ambition, how much art thou shrunk!
When that this body did contain a spirit,
A kingdom for it was too small a bound;
But now, two paces of the vilest earth
Is room enough.   This earth, that bears thee dead,
Bears not alive so brave a gentleman.
If thou wert sensible of courtesy,
I should not make so dear a show of zeal;
But let my favors hide thy mangled face;
And even in thy behalf, I'll thank myself
For doing these fair rites of tenderness.
Adieu, and take thy praise with thee to heaven!
Thy ignominy sleep with thee in the grave,
But not remembered in thy epitaph!

Is there not a touch of Hamlet in this speech? Could the philosophic Dane have uttered more generous, thoughtful words? O how sincerely, how fervently we could apply these last lines to the Prince himself!

CHAPTER VII.

THE MERRY MEETING—THE DEER-STEALING ADVENTURE.

NOW comes the famous scene after the robbery, a scene which, besides being crammed with wit, humor, and jollity, gives such a vivid picture of the character whom we are endeavoring to identify with that of the Poet, that he who has read it a hundred times may well afford, in this new light, to read it again. Indeed, I trust that every one who reads this essay will henceforth read the entire play with much more insight, much more pleasure and satisfaction than he ever read it before.

Passing Falstaff's extraordinary account of his bravery, let me quote the concluding part of this marvellously interesting scene :

Prince. Well, breathe awhile, and then to it again; and when thou hast tired thyself in base comparisons, hear me speak but this.

Poins. Mark, Jack.

Prince. We two saw you four set on four; you bound them, and were masters of their wealth.— Mark now, how a plain tale shall put you down.— Then did we two set on you four: and, with a word, out-faced you from your prize, and have it; yea, and can show it you here in the house:—And Falstaff, you carried your guts away as nimbly, with as quick dexterity, and roared for mercy, and still ran and roared, as ever I heard bull-calf. What a slave art thou, to hack thy sword as thou hast done; and then say, it was in fight! What trick, what device, what starting-hole, canst thou now find out, to hide thee from this open and apparent shame?

Poins. Come, let's hear, Jack: what trick hast thou now?

Fal. By the Lord, I knew ye, as well as He that made ye. Why, hear ye, my masters: Was it for me to kill the heir-apparent? Should I turn upon the true prince? Why, thou knowest, I am as valiant as Hercules; but beware instinct: the lion will not touch the true prince. Instinct is a great matter; I was a coward on instinct. I shall think the better of myself and thee, during my life: I for a valiant lion, and thou for a true prince. But, by the Lord, lads, I am glad you have the money. —Hostess, clap to the doors; watch to-night, pray to-morrow.—Gallants, lads, boys, hearts of gold, all the titles of good fellowship come to you! What, shall we be merry? shall we have a play extempore?

Prince. Content;—and the argument shall be thy running away.

Fal. Ah! no more of that, Hal, an thou lovest me.

Enter Hostess.

Host. My lord the prince,—

Prince. How now, my lady the hostess? what say'st thou to me?

Host. Marry, my lord, there is a nobleman of the court at door would speak with you: he says, he comes from your father.

Prince. Give him as much as will make him a royal man, and send him back again to my mother.

Fal. What manner of man is he?

Host. An old man.

Fal. What doth gravity out of his bed at midnight?—Shall I give him his answer?

Prince. Pr'ythee, do, Jack.

Fal. 'Faith, and I'll send him packing. [*Exit.*

Prince. Now, sirs; by'r lady, you fought fair;—so did you, Peto; so did you, Bardolph: you are lions too, you ran away upon instinct, you will not touch the true prince; no,—fye!

Bard. 'Faith, I ran when I saw others run.

Prince. Tell me now in earnest, how came Falstaff's sword so hacked?

Peto. Why, he hacked it with his dagger; and

said he would swear truth out of England, but he would make you believe it was done in fight; and persuaded us to do the like.

Bard. Yea, and to tickle our noses with spear-grass to make them bleed : and then to beslubber our garments with it, and to swear it was the blood of true men. I did that I did not this seven year before ; I blushed to hear his monstrous devices.

Prince. O, villain, thou stolest a cup of sack eighteen years ago, and wert taken with the manner, and ever since thou hast blushed extempore ! Thou hadst fire and sword on thy side, and yet thou ran'st away. What instinct hadst thou for it?

Bard. My lord, do you see these meteors ? do you behold these exhalations?

Prince. I do.

Bard. What think you they portend ?

Prince. Hot livers and cold purses.

Bard. Choler, my lord, if rightly taken.

Prince. No, if rightly taken, halter.

Re-enter FALSTAFF.

Here comes lean Jack, here comes bare-bone. How now, my sweet creature of bombast? How long is't ago, Jack, since thou sawest thine own knee ?

Fal. My own knee ? when I was about thy years, Hal, I was not an eagle's talon in the waist ; I could have crept into any alderman's thumb-ring. A plague of sighing and grief ! it blows a man up like a bladder. There's villanous news abroad : here was Sir John Bracy from your father; you must to the court in the morning. That same mad fellow of the north, Percy; and he of Wales, that gave Amaimon the bastinado, and made Lucifer cuckold, and swore the devil his true liegeman upon the cross of a Welsh hook,—what, a plague, call you him?—

Poins. O, Glendower.

Fal. Owen, Owen; the same;—and his son-in-law, Mortimer; and old Northumberland; and that sprightly Scot of Scots, Douglas, that runs o'horseback up a hill perpendicular.

Prince. He that rides at high speed, and with his pistol kills a sparrow flying.

Fal. You have hit it.

Prince. So did he never the sparrow.

Fal. Well, that rascal hath good mettle in him; he will not run.

Prince. Why, what a rascal art thou then, to praise him so for running?

Fal. O'horseback, ye cuckoo! but, afoot, he will not budge a foot.

Prince. Yes, Jack, upon instinct.

Fal. I grant ye, upon instinct. Well, he is there too, and one Mordake, and a thousand blue-caps more. Worcester is stolen away to-night; thy father's beard is turned white with the news: you may buy land now as cheap as stinking mackerel.

Prince. Why, then, 'tis like, if there comes a hot June, and this civil buffeting hold, we shall buy maidenheads as they buy hob-nails, by the hundred.

Fal. By the mass, lad, thou sayest true; it is

like, we shall have good trading that way.—But tell me, Hal, art thou not horribly afeard? thou being heir-apparent, could the world pick thee out three such enemies again, as that fiend Douglas, that spirit Percy, and that devil Glendower? Art thou not horribly afraid? doth not thy blood thrill at it?

Prince. Not a whit, i'faith; I lack some of thy instinct.

Fal. Well, thou wilt be horribly chid to-morrow, when thou comest to thy father: if thou love me, practise an answer.

Prince. Do thou stand for my father, and examine me upon the particulars of my life.

Fal. Shall I? content :—This chair shall be my state, this dagger my scepter, and this cushion my crown.

Prince. Thy state is taken for a joint-stool, thy golden scepter for a leaden dagger, and thy precious rich crown, for a pitiful bald crown!

Fal. Well, an the fire of grace be not quite out of thee, now shalt thou be moved.—Give me a cup of sack, to make mine eyes look red, that it may be thought I have wept; for I must speak in passion, and I will do it in king Cambyses' vein.

Prince. Well, here is my leg.

Fal. And here is my speech :—Stand aside, nobility.

Host. This is excellent sport, i'faith.

Fal. Weep not, sweet queen, for trickling tears are vain.

Host. O, the father! how he holds his countenance!

Fal. For God's sake, lords, convey my tristful
queen,
For tears do stop the flood-gates of her eyes.

Host. O rare! he doth it as like one of these
harlotry players as I ever see.

Fal. Peace, good pint-pot; peace, good tickle-
brain.—Harry, I do not only marvel where thou
spendest thy time, but also how thou art accompanied: for though the camomile, the more it is
trodden on, the faster it grows, yet youth, the more
it is wasted, the sooner it wears. That thou art my
son, I have partly thy mother's word, partly my own
opinion; but chiefly, a villanous trick of thine eye,
and a foolish hanging of thy nether lip, that doth
warrant me. If then thou be son to me, here lies
the point;—Why, being son to me, art thou so
pointed at? Shall the blessed sun of heaven prove
a micher, and eat blackberries? a question not to
be asked. Shall the son of England prove a thief,
and take purses? a question to be asked. There
is a thing, Harry, which thou hast often heard of,
and it is known to many in our land by the name
of pitch: this pitch, as ancient writers do report,
doth defile; so doth the company thou keepest:
for, Harry, now I do not speak to thee in drink,
but in tears; not in pleasure, but in passion; not
in words only, but in woes also:—And yet there is
a virtuous man, whom I have often noted in thy
company, but I know not his name.

Prince. What manner of man, an it like your majesty?

Fal. A goodly portly man, i'faith, and a corpulent; of a cheerful look, a pleasing eye, and a most noble carriage ; and, as I think, his age some fifty, or by'r-lady, inclining to three-score; and now I remember me, his name is Falstaff: if that man should be lewdly given, he deceiveth me ; for, Harry, I see virtue in his looks. If then the tree may be known by the fruit, as the fruit by the tree, then, peremptorily I speak it, there is virtue in that Fal-staff : him keep with, the rest banish. And tell me now, thou naughty varlet, tell me, where hast thou been this month?

Prince. Dost thou speak like a king? Do thou stand for me, and I'll play my father.

Fal. Depose me ? if thou dost it half so gravely, so majestically, both in word and matter, hang me up by the heels for a rabbit-sucker, or a poulter's hare.

Prince. Well, here I am set.

Fal. And here I stand :—judge, my masters.

Prince. Now, Harry ! whence come you ?

Fal. My noble lord, from Eastcheap.

Prince. The complaints I hear of thee are grievous.

Fal. 'Sblood, my lord, they are false :—nay, I'll tickle ye for a young prince, i'faith.

Prince. Swearest thou, ungracious boy ? henceforth ne'er look on me. Thou art violently carried away from grace : there is a devil haunts thee, in the likeness of a fat old man: a tun of man is thy companion. Why dost thou converse with that trunk of humors, that bolting-hutch of beastliness, that swoln parcel of dropsies, that huge bombard of sack, that stuffed cloak-bag of guts, that roasted Manningtree ox with the pudding in his belly, that reverend vice, that gray iniquity, that father ruffian, that vanity in years? Wherein is he good, but to taste sack and drink it? wherein neat and cleanly, but to carve a capon and eat it? wherein cunning, but in craft? wherein crafty, but in villany? wherein villanous, but in all things? wherein worthy, but in nothing?

Fal. I would your grace would take me with you; whom means your grace?

Prince. That villanous abominable misleader of youth, Falstaff, that old white-bearded Satan.

Fal. My lord, the man I know.

Prince. I know thou dost.

Fal. But to say, I know more harm in him than in myself, were to say more than I know. That he is old (the more the pity) his white hairs do witness it: but that he is (saving your reverence) a whore-master, that I utterly deny. If sack and sugar be a fault, God help the wicked! If to be old and merry be a sin, then many an old host that I know is damned: if to be fat be to be hated, then Pharaoh's lean kine are to be loved. No, my good lord; banish Peto, banish Bardolph, banish Poins: but for sweet Jack Falstaff, kind Jack Falstaff, true Jack Falstaff, valiant Jack Falstaff, and therefore more

6

valiant, being as he is, old Jack Falstaff, banish not him thy Harry's company; banish plump Jack, and banish all the world.

Prince.   I do, I will.   [*A knocking heard.*
      [*Exeunt Hostess,* FRANCIS, *and* BARDOLPH.

Re-enter BARDOLPH, *running.*

Bard.   O, my lord, my lord! the sheriff, with a most monstrous watch, is at the door.

Fal.   Out, you rogue! play out the play: I have much to say in the behalf of that Falstaff.

Re-enter Hostess, hastily.

Host.   O Jesu, my lord, my lord!—

Fal.   Heigh! heigh! the devil rides upon a fiddlestick: What's the matter?

Host.   The sheriff and all the watch are at the door: they are come to search the house. Shall I let them in?

Fal.   Dost thou hear, Hal? never call a true piece of gold, a counterfeit: thou art essentially mad, without seeming so.

Prince.   And thou a natural coward, without instinct.

Fal.   I deny your *major;* if you will deny the sheriff, so; if not, let him enter: if I become not a cart as well as another man, a plague on my bringing up! I hope I shall as soon be strangled with a halter as another.

Prince.   Go, hide thee behind the arras ;—the rest

walk up above.   Now, my masters, for a true face
and a good conscience.

Fal.   Both which I have had : but their date is
out, and therefore I'll hide me.

> [*Exeunt all but the* PRINCE *and* POINS.

Prince.   Call in the sheriff.—

Enter Sheriff and Carrier.

Now, master Sheriff, what's your will with me ?

Sher.   First, pardon me, my lord.   A hue and cry
Hath followed certain men into this house.

Prince.   What men ?

Sher.   One of them is well known, my gracious
    lord,
A gross fat man.

Car.   As fat as butter.

Prince.   The man, I do assure you, is not here ;
For I myself at this time have employed him.
And, Sheriff, I will engage my word to thee,
That I will, by to-morrow dinner-time,
Send him to answer thee, or any man,
For any thing he shall be charged withal :
And so let me entreat you leave the house.

Sher.   I will, my lord.   There are two gentlemen
Have in this robbery lost three hundred marks.

Prince.   It may be so : if he have robbed these
    men,
He shall be answerable ; and so, farewell.

Sher.   Good night, my noble lord.

Prince.   I think it is good-morrow ; is it not ?

Sher.   Indeed, my lord, I think it be two oclock.
         [*Exeunt Sheriff and Carrier.*

Prince. This oily rascal is known as well as Paul's. Go call him forth.

Poins. Falstaff ! Fast asleep behind the arras, and snorting like a horse.

Prince.   Hark, how hard he fetches breath ! Search his pockets. [POINS *searches.*] What hast thou found ?

Poins.   Nothing but papers, my lord.

Prince.   Let's see what they be : read them.

Poins.   Item, A capon, 2*s.* 2*d.*

Item, Sauce, 4*d.*

Item, Sack, two gallons, 5*s.* 8*d.*

Item, Anchovies, and sack after supper, 2*s.* 6*d.*

Item, Bread, a half-penny.

Prince.   O monstrous ! but one half-pennyworth of bread to this intolerable deal of sack !—What there is else, keep close; we'll read it at more advantage : there let him sleep till day. I'll to the court in the morning : we must all to the wars, and thy place shall be honorable. I'll procure this fat rogue a charge of foot; and, I know, his death will be a march of twelve-score. The money shall be paid back again with advantage. Be with me betimes in the morning; and so good-morrow, Poins.

Poins.   Good-morrow, good my lord.

Now let the reader peruse Halliwell's account of the deer-stealing adventure, and judge for himself if it have not given rise to this scene in the play, as well as to the satire on Sir Thomas Lucy, which shall be given presently.

"The public records contain many notices of deer-stealing. In 1583 Lord Berkeley issued a bill in the Star Chamber against twenty persons who had hunted deer unlawfully in his forests. The answer of William Waare, one of the defendants, is preserved in the Chapter House, Westminster, xciv. 24, and he confesses having killed a doe, but, notwithstanding that admission, asserts that the proceedings against him were malicious and uncalled-for. Fosbroke (Hist. Glouc. i. 125) mentions an anecdote tending to show that respectable persons in the county of Gloucestershire, adjoining Warwickshire, were not ashamed of the practice of deer-stealing. Several attorneys and others, 'all men of metall, and good woodmen, *I mean old notorious deer-stealers*, well armed, came in the night-time to Michaelwood with deer-nets and dogs, to steale deer.' Falstaff asks, 'Am I a woodman?' Can it have been an old cant term for a deer-stealer? If so, Falstaff's speech may allude to what is stated in the commencement of the *Merry Wives of Windsor*.

" Shakespeare is said, on good authority, to have been implicated in a frolic of this kind; and, although the earliest notice of the tale was not penned till nearly eighty years after the death of the poet, yet the person who recorded it resided in a neighboring county, and being a clergyman, with no motive whatever to mislead, his testimony is of great value.   The Rev. William Fulman, who died in 1688, bequeathed his biographical collections to his friend, the Rev. Richard Davies, rector of Sapperton in Gloucestershire, who made several additions to them.   Davies died in 1708, and these manuscripts were presented to the library of Corpus Christi College, Oxford, where they are still preserved.   Under the article *Shakespeare*, Fulman made very few notes, and those of little importance ; but Davies inserted the curious information, so important in the consideration of the deer-stealing story.   The following is a complete copy of what the manuscript contains respecting Shakespeare :

"'William Shakespeare was born at Stratford-upon-Avon in Warwickshire, about 1563–4.   Much given to all unluckinesse in stealing venison and rabbits, particularly from Sr. . . . . Lucy, who had him oft whipt and sometimes imprisoned, and at last made him fly his native country, to his great advancement; but his revenge was so great, that he is his Justice Clodpate, and calls him a great man, and that, in allusion to his name, bore three louses rampant for his arms.   From an actor of plays he became a composer.   He dyed April 23d, 1616, ætat. 53, probably at Stratford, for there he is buryed, and hath a monument (*Dugd.* p. 520), on which he lays a heavy curse upon any one who shal remoove his bones.   He dyed a papist.'"

Rowe, who wrote the first account of Shakespeare's life, published in 1709, ninety-three years after the Poet's death, thus recounts the deer-stealing episode :

" In this kind of settlement Shakespeare continued for some time, till an extravagance that he was guilty of, forced him both out of his country and that way of living which he had taken up; and, though it seemed at first to be a blemish upon his good manners, and a misfortune to him, yet it afterwards happily proved the occasion of exerting one of the greatest geniuses that ever was known in dramatic poetry. He had, by a misfortune common enough to young fellows, fallen into ill company; and among them some, that made a frequent practice of deer-stealing, engaged him with them more than once in robbing a park that belonged to Sir Thomas Lucy, of Charlecote, near Stratford. For this he was prosecuted by that gentleman, as he thought, somewhat too severely; and, in order to revenge that ill usage, he made a ballad upon him. And though this, probably the first essay of his poetry, be lost, yet it is said to have been so very bitter, that it redoubled the prosecution against him, to that degree that he was obliged to leave his business and family in Warwickshire for some time, and shelter himself in London."

Does not this look like the quarry whence the above scenes were taken?

Did not the Poet simply improve real life by the colors of his imagination?   All good scenes in fiction have a substratum of truth in them ; all the best characters of our first-class novelists and dramatists are drawn from life.   Mr. Halliwell, after quoting the above passage from the Rev. Richard Davies, continues :

" This testimony has been doubted, because no such character as Clodpate occurs in any of Shake-peare's plays ; but it was a generic term of the time for a foolish person, and that Davies so used it, there can, I think, be little doubt.   In the MS. account of Warwickshire, 1693, before quoted, the writer calls the judge of the Warwick assizes Mr. Justice Clodpate, intending to characterize him as an ignorant, stupid man.   The 'three louses ram-pant' refer to the arms actually borne by Lucy. The 'dozen white luces' in the play is merely one of Slender's mistakes.   At all events, here we have the earliest explanation of the remarkable satirical allusions to the Lucy family at the commencement of the *Merry Wives of Windsor.*   ' I will make a Star Chamber matter of it,' says Justice Shallow ; and we have just seen that the offence of deer-stealing was referred to that arbitrary court.   ' You have beaten my men, killed my deer, and broke open my lodge.'   Davies tells us, moreover, what we should have believed independently of his authority, that

Sir Thomas Lucy was ridiculed under one of his characters. That character is Justice Shallow, and the satire is by no means confined to one play. There can be little doubt but that the exquisite descriptions of a country justice of the peace in the second part of *Henry IV.* are in some degree founded upon Sir Thomas Lucy. When Falstaff says, 'If the young dace be a bait for the old pike, I see no reason, in the law of nature, but I may snap at him,' we see a direct personal allusion, a luce being merely a full-grown pike. Harrison, in his 'Description of England,' p. 224, says, 'The pike, as he ageth, receiveth diverse names, as from a frie to a gilthed, from a gilthed to a pod, from a pod to a jacke, from a jacke to a pickerell, from a pickerell to a pike, and last of all to a luce.' Shallow's declaration, 'I am, sir, under the king, in some authority,' the constant ebullitions of importance where so much is inadequate in his nature to support it, and touches that give his whole character the air of a semi-ludicrous creation, would more severely wound an individual, if Sir Thomas was recognized by such foibles, than the keenest verses attached to the gate of Charlecote Park. I trust that in adopting this view of the case, believing the account given by Davies to shadow the truth, I am not falling into the error of particularizing a generic character. I am too well aware that Shakespeare's inventions were 'not of an age, but for all time;' but in this instance we have palpable evidence of an allusion to an individual, a neighbor of Shake-

speare's, introduced in a manner to leave no room
for hesitating to believe that a retaliating satire was
intended. Again, observe how severe is Falstaff
on Shallow's administration of justice, on the ' semblable coherence of his men's spirits and his.'
Davy's interceding for his friend Visor is one of the
keenest satires of the kind to be found in Shakespeare."

Then Mr. Halliwell shows the remarkable fact that Shakespeare "adopted the
names of his characters from his neighbors in Warwickshire."   Even Shakespeare's father is found, among the
records of Stratford, to be associated
with one named Fluellen and another
named Bardolph in a fine for not attend-
ing church !   This, certainly, is Bardol-
phean enough ; and, for aught we know,
he may be the very prototype of the red-
nosed companion of Falstaff.   Why,
therefore, should it be thought incredible
that he should draw the likenesses as
well as adopt the names of his neighbors?   Why, should it be thought incredible that he should paint others
whom he knew besides Sir Thomas Lucy,
and especially one living character, whom

he knew best of all? I have no doubt that a Stratfordian would not only have discovered Sir Thomas Lucy in Justice Shallow, but would have recognized in Falstaff and Bardolph two other well-known Warwickshire characters. And if he were an intimate friend, he would have recognized the Poet himself in the Prince, and enjoyed the play even more than the Londoners;—for Shakespeare no more invented men than he invented plots; he adopted those whom he found among his neighbors and associates, and sometimes the very names along with the characters. In fact, I think he wrote the whole play with real names all the way through, and only changed them when the play was copied. And is not this item, the examining of Falstaff's pockets, such a thing as the character-studying poet might be guilty of? Could anything be more natural to a man who could "drink with any tinker in his own language," play such fantastic tricks with tapsters, and disguise himself as a "drawer" or pot-boy in a practical joke?

Who that knows anything of tavern-life has not seen such a thing?   Between the poet and one of his boon companions nothing could be more natural ; especially when we consider what use he made of it, and how completely he exposed the old fox when he complained of being robbed of "four bonds of forty pounds apiece, and a seal-ring of his grandfather's : " .

Prince. . . . . Charge an honest woman with picking thy pocket ! Why, thou impudent embossed rascal, if there were anything in thy pocket but tavern reckonings, memorandums of bawdy-houses, and one poor pennyworth of sugar-candy to make thee long-winded ; if thy pocket were enriched with any other injuries but these, I am a villain.   And yet you will stand to it ; you will not pocket up wrong : art thou not ashamed ?

Fal.   Dost thou hear, Hal ? thou knowest, in the state of innocency Adam fell ; and what should poor Jack Falstaff do in the days of villany ?   Thou seest I have more flesh than another man, and therefore more frailty.—You confess, then, you picked my pocket ?

Prince.   It seems so by the story.

I have always looked upon the Gads-hill exploit and its sequel as but another version of one of Shakespeare's own deer-stealing adventures, and upon Falstaff as a portrait of one of his early associates in these adventures. The thing looks too real to be an invention; especially as Shakespeare never invented plots, but seized upon those that he found at hand. Falstaff is obviously a picture of one of those witty roysterers with whom he passed many a merry hour in the days when he

" went gypsying, a long time ago ; "

one of those " young fellows " into whose " ill company " he had fallen ; and I am sure he took as much delight in painting the picture as we take in the observation of it.

Of course, I know that Falstaff (or Oldcastle, which was the name first given him) is a character in history; but there is no more resemblance between the Falstaff of history and the Falstaff of Shakespeare than between chalk and cheese. Sir John Oldcastle, the good Lord Cobham, was a person of an entirely different character from Falstaff; and the Fastolfe of the French wars is a man of whom we know almost nothing. In fact, these historical characters are mere skeletons or shadows of men; while Shakespeare's Falstaff is a real, substantial man, full of all that is living and life-like in spirit and conversation, witty, jovial, genial, sensible,—perhaps the most real, living and substantial character in literature. Such a character could not be taken from any musty historical records, but from the author's intimate personal acquaintance; he was a man with whom he had lived, laughed, and talked in familiar daily intercourse. No real live character is ever conjured up from the imagination; such a character *must* be taken from life. Who that has mixed much among men has not known such a man as Falstaff? Yet who among men is able to paint him like the great master?

Indeed, I think Shakespeare had, like most good writers of fiction, a living representative for nearly every character he drew : that is, he idealized living or real characters, and made them show themselves more completely themselves than they ever actually did in life. A word or an incident often unfolded to him the whole soul of a man, and when he wanted to portray him, he showed him as he saw him ; he knew how he would think, talk, and act on given occasions, and painted him accordingly. Thus many a scene in which Falstaff appears is not an actual transcript of what occurred, but of what would occur were he actually in that situation. "I have little doubt," says Washington Irving, "that in early life, when running like an unbroken colt about the neighborhood of Stratford, Shakespeare was to be found in the company of all kinds of anomalous characters [is it not a peculiarity of genius to seek out such characters?]; that he associated with all the madcaps of the place, and was one of those unlucky urchins, at mention of whom old men shake their heads, and predict that they will one day come to the gallows." Precisely. So did people predict of Prince Henry ; so have people predicted of many another man of genius. Shakespeare well remembered these predictions ; and he makes the Prince determine, like him, to disappoint those who "did forethink his fall."

To show that the Poet was in the habit of portraying real characters and real scenes, let me quote a striking passage from Halliwell-Phillipps' "Outlines of the Life of Shakespeare," wherein he describes the origin of Christopher Sly in the Induction to the *Taming of the Shrew.* "That delicious episode," says he, "presents us with a fragment of the rural life with which Shakespeare himself must have been familiar in his native county. With such animated power is it written, that we almost appear to personally witness the affray between Marian Hacket, the fat ale-wife of Wincot, and Christopher Sly ; to see the nobleman on his return from the chase discovering the insensible drunkard ; and to hear the strolling actors make the offer of professional services, which was requited by the cordial welcome to the buttery. Wincot is a secluded hamlet near Stratford-on-Avon, and there is an old tradition that the ale-house frequented by Sly was often resorted to by Shakespeare for the sake of diverting himself with a fool who belonged to a neighboring mill. [Could anything be more like the conduct of the Prince?] Stephen Sly, one of the tinker's friends or relatives, was a known character at Stratford-on-Avon, and is several times mentioned in the records of that town. This fact, taken in conjunction with the references to Wilmecote and Burton-on-the-Heath, definitely prove that the scene of the Induction was intended to be in the neighborhood of Stratford-on-Avon, the water-mill tradition leading to the belief that little Wilmecote, the part of the hamlet nearest to the Poet's native town, is the Wincot alluded to in the comedy."

Now, as Justice Shallow is universally acknowledged to be the portrait of a Stratfordian, and as I wish to let the reader see the Visor satire and the truth of Mr. Halliwell's conclusions, I think it worth his while for him to take a glance at the character, as presented in the Second Part of *Henry IV.*, Act V.

SCENE I.—Gloucestershire.   A Hall in Shallow's House.

Enter SHALLOW, FALSTAFF, BARDOLPH, *and Page.*

Shal. By cock and pye, sir, you shall not away to-night.—What, Davy, I say!

Fal. You must excuse me, master Robert Shallow.

Shal. I will not excuse you; you shall not be excused; excuses shall not be admitted; there is no excuse shall serve; you shall not be excused.— Why, Davy!

Enter DAVY.

Davy. Here, sir.

Shal. Davy, Davy, Davy,—let me see, Davy; let me see:—yea, marry, William cook, bid him come hither.—Sir John, you shall not be excused.

Davy. Marry, sir, thus:—those warrants cannot be served: and, again, sir,—shall we sow the headland with wheat?

Shal. With red wheat, Davy. But for William cook;—Are there no young pigeons?

Davy. Yes, sir.—Here is now the smith's note, for shoeing, and for plough-irons.

Shal. Let it be cast up, and paid.—Sir John, you shall not be excused.

Davy. Now, sir, a new link to the bucket must

needs be had.—And, sir, do you mean to stop any of William's wages, about the sack he lost the other day at Hinckley fair?

Shal. He shall answer it :—Some pigeons, Davy; a couple of short legged hens; a joint of mutton; and any pretty little tiny kickshaws, tell William cook.

Davy. Doth the man of war stay all night, sir?

Shal. Yes, Davy, I will use him well. A friend i'the court is better than a penny in purse. Use his men well, Davy; for they are arrant knaves, and will backbite.

Davy. No worse than they are backbitten, sir; for they have marvelous foul linen.

Shal. Well conceited, Davy. About thy business, Davy.

Davy. I beseech you, sir, to countenance William Visor of Wincot, against Clement Perkes of the hill.

Shal. There are many complaints, Davy, against that Visor; that Visor is an arrant knave, on my knowledge.

Davy. I grant your worship, that he is a knave, sir; but yet, God forbid, sir, but a knave should have some countenance at his friend's request. An honest man, sir, is able to speak for himself, when a knave is not. I have served your worship truly, sir, this eight years; and if I cannot once or twice in a quarter bear out a knave against an honest man, I have but a very little credit with your worship. The knave is mine honest friend, sir; there-

fore, I beseech your worship, let him be counte-
nanced.

Shal.   Go to; I say, he shall have no wrong.
Look about, Davy.   [*Exit* DAVY.]   Where are you,
Sir John?   Come, off with your boots.—Give me
your hand, master Bardolph.

Bard.   I am glad to see your worship.

Shal.   I thank thee with all my heart, kind master Bardolph :—and welcome, my tall fellow.   [*To
the Page.*]   Come, Sir John.   .   [*Exit* SHALLOW.

Fal.   I'll follow you, good master Robert Shallow.
Bardolph, look to our horses.   [*Exeunt* BARDOLPH
and Page.]   If I were sawed into quantities, I
should make four dozen of such bearded hermit's-
staves as master Shallow.   It is a wonderful thing
to see the semblable coherence of his men's spirits
and his : they, by observing him, do bear themselves like foolish justices ; he, by conversing with
them, is turned into a justice-like serving man ; their
spirits are so married in conjunction with the participation of society, that they flock together in consent, like so many wild-geese.   If I had a suit to
master Shallow, I would humor his men with the
imputation of being near their master : if to his men,
I would curry with master Shallow, that no man
could better command his servants.   It is certain,
that either wise bearing, or ignorant carriage, is
caught, as men take diseases, one of another : therefore, let men take heed of their company.   I will
devise matter enough out of this Shallow, to keep
Prince Harry in continual laughter, the wearing-out

of six fashions (which is four terms, or two actions), and he shall laugh without *intervallums*. O, it is much, that a lie, with a slight oath, and a jest, with a sad brow, will do with a fellow that never had the ache in his shoulders! O, you shall see him laugh till his face be like a wet cloak ill laid up.

Shal. [*Within*] Sir John!

Fal. I come, master Shallow; I come, master Shallow.

There is one point in the concluding part of the scene after the robbery that ought to be noticed—that in which the Prince for the first and only time acts unlike himself, and tells a deliberate falsehood.

> The man, I do assure you, is not here ;
> For I myself at this time have employed him.

It may be said, that this is merely a white lie, quite allowable in aristocratic circles, according to the morals of that day. But a lie is never allowable in the mouth of a gentleman, least of all in that of a prince. Nor is it a sufficient excuse to say the Prince had to do this to screen his companion and save him from prison. The Poet could have made him give some excuse without absolute falsehood ; but perhaps he wished to show that the Prince had not escaped altogether uninjured in associating with persons of questionable character. His conduct is a practical illustration of the words he subsequently puts in the mouth of Falstaff touching Justice Shallow : " It is certain, that either wise bearing or ignorant carriage is caught, as men take diseases one of another ; therefore, let men take heed of their company."   The Prince had just listened to and laughed immoderately at a batch of the most monstrous lies ; and lying, which had become the order of the night, was looked upon as mere fun. Might not Shakespeare have remembered that he too had " done those things which he ought not to have done, and left undone those things which he ought to have done ?" and, wishing to make the portrait complete, he set down the blotches as well as the graces.

CHAPTER VIII.

"TURNING PAST EVILS TO ADVANTAGES."

BUT perhaps the strongest evidence yet presented of the truth of my theory, is that displayed in the Fourth Act, Fourth Scene, of the Second Part of *Henry IV.* I beg the reader carefully to note, in this scene, the king's characterization of the Prince, and especially the Earl of Warwick's account of the *motives* which induced him to select such company as he keeps.

Westminster. A Room in the Palace.
Enter the King, his sons CLARENCE *and* HUMPHREY, *the Earl of* WARWICK, *and others.*

King. Now, lords, if God doth give successful end
To this debate that bleedeth at our doors,
We will our youth lead on to higher fields,
And draw no swords but what are sanctified.
Our navy is addressed, our power collected,

Our substitutes in absence well invested,
And everything lies level to our wish :
Only we want a little personal strength,
And pause us, till these Rebels now afoot,
Come underneath the yoke of government.

 War. Both which we doubt not but your majesty
Shall soon enjoy.

 King.   Humphrey, my son of Gloster,
Where is the prince, your brother ?

 Humph. I think he's gone to hunt, my lord, at
    Windsor.

 King. And how accompanied ?

 Humph.   I do not know, my lord.

 King. Is not his brother, Thomas of Clarence,
    with him ?

 Humph. No, my good lord ; he's in presence
    here.

 Clar. What would my lord and father ?

 King. Nothing but well to thee, Thomas of
    Clarence.

How chance thou art not with the prince, thy
    brother ?
He loves thee, and thou dost neglect him, Thomas.
Thou hast a better place in his affection
Than all thy brothers : cherish it, my boy ;
And noble offices thou mayst effect
Of mediation, after I am dead,
Between his greatness and thy other brethren :
Therefore omit him not ; blunt not his love,
Nor lose the good advantage of his grace,
By seeming cold or careless of his will.

For he is gracious if he be observed:
He hath a tear for pity, and a hand
Open as day for melting charity:
Yet, notwithstanding, being incens'd, he's flint;
*As humorous * as winter, and as sudden*
As flaws † congealed in the spring of day.
His temper, therefore, must be well observed:
Chide him for faults, and do it reverently,
When you perceive his blood inclined to mirth;
But, being moody, give him line and scope,
Till that his passions, like a whale on ground,
Confound themselves with working. Learn this, Thomas,
And thou shalt prove a shelter to thy friends,
A hoop of gold, to bind thy brothers in:
That the united vessel of their blood,
Mingled with venom of suggestion,
(As force per force, the age will pour it in,)
Shall never leak, though it do work as strong
As aconitum, or rash gunpowder.

   Clar. I shall observe him with all care and love.

   King. Why art thou not at Windsor with him, Thomas?

   Clar. He is not there to-day; he dines in London.

   King. And how accompanied? Canst thou tell that?

---

* Capricious.

† *Flaws* are the small blades of ice which are struck on the edges of water in winter mornings.—*Edwards.*

Clar.   With Poins, and other his continual followers.

King.   Most subject is the fattest soil to weeds;
And he, the noble image of my youth,
Is overspread with them.   Therefore, my grief
Stretches itself beyond the hour of death:
The blood weeps from my heart, when I do shape,
In forms imaginary, the unguided days,
And rotten times, that you shall look upon,
When I am sleeping with my ancestors.
For when his headstrong riot hath no curb,
When rage and hot blood are his counsellors,
When means and lavish manners meet together,
O! with what wings shall his affections * fly,
Towards fronting peril and opposed decay!

War.   My gracious lord, you look beyond him
quite:

The prince but studies his companions,
Like a strange tongue; wherein, to gain the language,
'Tis needful that the most immodest word
Be looked upon, and learned; which, once attained,
Your highness knows, comes to no further use,
But to be known and hated.   So, like gross terms,
The prince will, in the perfectness of time,
Cast off his followers; and *their memory*
Shall as a pattern or a measure live
By which his grace must mete the lives of others,
Turning past evils to advantages.

---

* Passions.

Could anything be more plain ?   Is it
not evident from what we know of his
history, that he here shows how he himself "turned past evils to advantages?"
how he mixed among men, even of the
meaner sort, in order to "mete the lives
of others," and turn his knowledge of
their language and behavior to advantage in his art?   Was it not thus that he
"held the mirror up to nature?"   Did
he not indeed make use of their memory
as "a pattern or a measure" whereby to
"mete the lives of others?"   Thus had
he turned the evil of his own early life
to advantage ; thus had he enriched the
world with the most natural and most
entertaining characters in literature; thus
had he coined his own experience into
golden lessons of life and conduct for
all mankind.   How could he otherwise
have learned so much about all classes
of men ?   How could he otherwise have
acquired such minute and exact knowledge of the habits, manners, character,
and language of the lowest as well as
of the highest people ?   His friendship

with Southampton, Montgomery and Pembroke served him in no less good stead than his friendship with the humblest people whom he knew. "His mind educated itself, not by early study or instruction, but by active listening and rapid apprehension."

Let the reader observe how well the Earl's account of the Prince's conduct agrees with the Bishop's description of the manner in which he obtained his knowledge :

The strawberry grows underneath the nettle,
And wholesome berries thrive and ripen best
Neighbored by fruit of baser quality ;
And so the Prince obscured his contemplation
Under the veil of wildness.

The Prince himself, when he has " turned away his former self," and is no longer "the thing he was," refers to his early experiences in the same light. The Dauphin having sent him, shortly after he had ascended the throne, a set of tennis-balls, as a derisive fling at his early associations, the Prince thus answers him :

> And we understand him well,
> How he comes o'er us with our wilder days,
> *Not measuring what use we made of them.*

And the wiser of the French king's counsellors, on learning from the ambassadors the behavior of the English king, saw that he was a man not to be measured by the indications of his youth:

> *Dauphin.* For, my good lord, she is so idly
>   king'd,
> Her scepter so fantastically borne,
> By a vain, giddy, shallow, humorous youth,
> That fear attends her not.
> *Constable.*   O peace, Prince Dauphin !
> You are too much mistaken in this king.
> Question your Grace the late ambassadors,—
> With what great state he heard their embassy;
> How well supplied with noble counsellors;
> How modest in exception, and withal
> How terrible in constant resolution,—
> And you shall find, *his vanities, forespent,*
> *Were but the outside of the Roman Brutus,*
> *Covering discretion with a coat of folly.*

How significant is that phrase, " covering discretion with a coat of folly !" Can we not imagine that Shakespeare, the *actor* as well as author, did this thing?

Consider for a moment how the wisest
man of antiquity acquired his wisdom:

"I sought in mine heart to give myself unto
wine, yet acquainting mine heart with wisdom; and
to lay hold on folly, till I might see what *was* that
good for the sons of men which they should do under the heaven all the days of their life.

"I made me great works; I builded me houses;
I planted me vineyards; I made me gardens and
orchards; and I planted trees in them of all kinds
of fruits:

"I made me pools of water, to water therewith
the wood that bringeth forth trees:

"I got me servants and maidens [concubines],
and had servants born in my house:

"I gathered me also silver and gold, and the peculiar treasure of kings, and of the provinces; I got
me men-singers and women-singers, and the delights of the sons of men, as musical instruments,
and these of all sorts:

"So I was great, and increased more than all that
were before me in Jerusalem: also my wisdom re-
mained with me.

"And whatsoever mine eyes desired I kept not
from them; I withheld not my heart from any joy;
for my heart rejoiced in all my labor: and this was
my portion of all my labor.

"Then I looked on all the works that my hands
had wrought, and on the labor that I had labored

to do : and behold, all was vanity and vexation of spirit, and there was no profit under the sun.

"Then I turned myself to behold wisdom, and madness, and folly :

"And I saw that wisdom excelleth folly as far as light excelleth darkness."

All which strongly exemplifies the truth which I have already shown, that it is not books, nor classical studies, that make men great poets and great novelists, but actual experimental knowledge.

I do not mean by all this to infer that a young man should, to become acquainted with the world and acquire wisdom, cultivate the acquaintance of lewd and wicked people, and do wicked things. God forbid! but when he has become a man, and has attained some firmness of character, it will not be amiss for him to mix among people of all classes with the view of becoming personally acquainted with their character. There is nothing like experimental knowledge, especially for the purposes of art. Outside of this, nothing will help him so much as the plays of Shakespeare, who seems to have known men and women better than any other human being that ever lived.

"Most subject are the fattest soils to weeds." What fat soils and what weeds were found in many of the most distinguished men in history! Need I mention, for instance, Cæsar, Antony, Alexander, St. Augustine, Marlowe, Steele, Mirabeau, Rousseau and Fox? A whole catalogue of such men might be made out. If ever there was a fat soil, it was that of Shakespeare, and we know from his Sonnets, and from various other sources, that the weeds were not lacking.

M. Taine, who, like so many others, discovers Shakespeare in *Hamlet*, finds most of the materials of his life in the Sonnets. Hamlet may indeed be Shakespeare in some part of his life; in those days when he was most "sicklied o'er with the pale cast of thought;" when the origin of things and the mystery of existence occupied his mind in an uncommon degree; and when, as some suppose, he had suffered some terrible stroke of fate; —but the Shakespeare of the Sonnets belongs to the earlier period, to that part of his life in which he was beginning to tear himself away from the Siren circle that seems to have held him fast so long, and when he was turning toward nobler and greater things :

Alas ! 'tis true ; I have gone here and there
And made myself a motley to the view ;
Gored mine own thoughts ;
Sold cheap what is most dear.

O for my sake, do thou with Fortune chide,
  The guilty goddess of my harmful deeds,
That did not better for my life provide,
  Than public means, which public manners
    breeds.

Thence comes it that my name receives a brand,
  And almost thence my nature is subdued
To what it works in, like the dyer's hand.
  Pity me then . . . . . .
Whilst, like a willing patient, I will drink
  Potions of eysel.

These lines look, indeed, as Mr. Armitage Brown thinks, as if they were addressed to one of his noble friends, perhaps the Earl of Southampton, lamenting the unhappy associations and unfavor-

8

able reputation of the stage ; and it is clear that, mixing in this high and noble society, he felt a stigma cast on his name as an actor. During all his life, and through all his works, he entertained a high respect for the nobility, and finally endeavored to become one of them himself.

The following passage is of the same tenor, sorrowing over the disgraceful and outcast state of his profession in men's eyes, and sighing to be "like one more rich in hope;" but still displaying the mental agonies of one who was struggling toward better things :

When in disgrace with Fortune and men's eyes,
  I all alone beweep my outcast state,
And trouble deaf Heaven with my bootless cries;
  And look upon myself, and curse my fate,
Wishing me like to one more rich in hope,
    Featured like him, like him with friends possessed . . . .
With what I most enjoy contented least;
    Yet in these thoughts myself almost despising.
Sonnet 91.

Does not this look like inward disgust

at vulgar and low associations, and remorse for the part he had played among
low and inferior people?

It is evident that his associations with
the nobility had cast a fascination over
him, and he wished he were one of them;
a wish which, as we shall see, never entirely left him. Let any young man who
has had to work hard for a living, who
has experienced all the ills of poverty
and severe toil, suddenly find himself on
an honorable footing among refined and
noble people, surrounded with all the
elegances of wealth, culture, and ease,
with ample time and means for study,
and he too, however philosophic in
character, will wish himself "like one
more rich in hope, featured like him, like
him with friends possessed." After the
very hardest kind of experience in his
youth, the writer suddenly found himself,
at twenty-five, a teacher of languages in
an aristocratic school in Germany, surrounded by people of refinement and culture, and with a handsome salary for giving a few lessons a day in his native

tongue. How keenly he appreciated the change and how much he envied those whose youth was so much more favored than his own ! He would willingly, had circumstances permitted, have passed his life in this delightful situation.

The first lines in the last quotation seem obviously to refer to that early period in which Shakespeare travelled with his company from town to town, making himself " a motley to the view." No doubt he had served a severe and bitter apprenticeship in the hard-faring and soul-trying profession of the actor ; he had endured the scoffs and jeers of those who derided his calling, and was probably severely criticised by people who knew nothing of his art, and who little suspected that this young actor was to become the regenerator and ornament of the English stage and of English literature. Might not that line,

" With what I most enjoy, contented least,"

refer to the fact, that although he loved the drama, he was ill-content with the parts he had to play, with the dramas in which he played, and with the people before whom or with whom he played ? *

Oh that some Boswell, some scribbling gossip who knew the man, had only put down what he knew of him ! Oh that Burbage or Ben Jonson had only told us

---

* Among the disputations for degrees at Oxford, in 1593, one was on the question, "Are players infamous?" And it seems they were decided to be so. (Clark's Register of the University.) Whether the players were infamous or not, these Oxfordians certainly made themselves so, by coming to such a decision. How could a great dramatic Poet come out of such a crowd?

Such, however, was, among certain classes, the sentiment of the age. Even in the Poet's own town of Stratford, the Corporation took stringent measures, in 1602 and 1611, to prevent the performance of plays therein. There reigned then certainly a mayor who "knew not Joseph." M. Taine tells us, the actor's profession was at that time "degraded by the brutalities of the crowd,—who not seldom would stone the actors, —and by the severities of the magistrates, who would sometimes condemn them to lose their ears."

Some of my younger readers may wonder why the players of that day are always spoken of as "his Majesty's servants," or as "the Lord So-and-So's servants." Why, if they could not get some protection, as the servants of some great man, they would be arrested and imprisoned as vagrants !

These are the things that show us what the " good old times " were. Is it any wonder that the learned folk did not think it worth while to take any notice of a "mere player" and playwright? They were beneath notice.

something of his early struggles, his dis-
appointments, his defeats, and his suc-
cesses !   If some diarist of that day,
some Pepys or Evelyn, had only noted
his sayings and doings, how much his
notes would have been prized ! Little
did they imagine who knew the man, and
who wrote voluminously of the king and
his courtiers, that they overlooked the
real king of men, the most princely soul
of that or any age, and wrote only of his
satellites ! Not that we need a Boswell
to tell us what manner of man Shakespeare was ; not that we need any such
intimate revealings as Boswell gave of
Johnson in order to understand his character ;—but to settle the idle talk of those
silly dreamers who, unable to discover
the man in his works, are bent upon having all the details of his private life, if
not in his own life, at least in those of
another. You may start any doctrine
or proposition you please ; you may an-
nounce yourself the apostle of the most
absolute rhodomontade that ever entered

the human brain ; and if you only scream long and loud enough, you will find a host of followers and believers. In every age and in every country there is a class of crotchety, cranky people, who are so eager for novelties and oddities, that they will swallow anything that tickles the palate and ministers to a diseased appetite.

How often have I regretted that, in those instances where the Poet's name was mentioned by one of his contemporaries, something was not said of his looks, his manner, or his character! Here is one of them. Most of the great commentators on Shakespeare's plays have contended that, from internal evidence, *Measure for Measure* must have been composed between 1609 and 1612; but it is now known that it was played before James the First, at Somerset House, in 1604. For this knowledge we are indebted to Mr. Tylney, who was Master of the Revels at this time, and who, in his account of the expenses for this year, has this entry : " By His Majesty's Players : on St. Stephen's night, in the Hall, a play called ' Measure for Measure,' by Mr. Shaxberd."

What a chance Tylney lost for grateful immortality ! The mere mention of the name of the playwright, whose name he could not spell, has preserved his for three hundred years, and will probably preserve it for many hundred more. But what a precious thing he would have conferred on us had he taken the trouble to make the acquaintance of " Mr. Shaxberd," and noted his ways and sayings, or said something interesting of him, along with this item ! How much we would have been indebted to him if he had only written as much as I have written here, on this page, about this humble playwright, whose name he knew not how to spell ! O young man, do not fail, when you come in contact with genius, to use your eyes and ears well, and to make some record of what you have seen and heard ; for you may thus not only confer a boon on posterity, but a pleasing immortality on yourself ! Who would not like to have his name linked in immortal association with that of the gentle Shakespeare, the sweet bard of Avon !

CHAPTER IX.

THE INCIDENTS OF SHAKESPEARE'S LIFE— HIS CONVERSATION—HIS WORKS.

THE stray notices of Shakespeare found here and there in the writers of his time, showing when he probably wrote such a play, when he stopped at such a place or played such a character, when he had so many shares in the theater, or bought such a piece of land, have very little to do in exhibiting to us the man Shakespeare, the poet whose works we read with so much admiration. It is the conversation, the thoughts, feelings, hopes and fears, aims and objects of a man that show us what he is; and the known incidents of Shakespeare's life show us few, if any, of these things. We know little of the man except what we find in his writings. But he is not so peculiar in this respect as many imagine.

" The great dramatist," says Mr. Halliwell-Phillipps, " participates in the fate of
most of his literary contemporaries ; for if
a collection of the known facts relating
to all of them were tabularly arranged, it
would be found that the number of the
ascertained particulars of his life reached
at least the average."   What do the details which we have of Massinger's life
show us of the man who wrote *A New
Way to pay Old Debts?*   What do the few
unhappy stories of Otway's career show
us of the man who wrote *Venice Preserved?*   What do these things show us
of the daily life and conversation of these
men ?   The men who wrote these plays
were quite different men from those who
are described as having eaten at such a
place, drunk at such another, and starved
at such another.   The man of genius is,
in the composition of his works, and in
the best moments of his social life, a
burning torch, shedding light on all
around, an inspired prophet and preacher,
bringing forth, with radiant feature and
beaming eye, things new and old for the

edification and delectation of mankind. And when his work is done, and he engages in the ordinary affairs of life, he becomes again a common mortal, thinking, speaking, acting, eating and drinking like any other common mortal. The men we see in the biographies are often poor wretched creatures, seeking or suing for bread among people who did not understand or appreciate them, and displaying nothing to identify them with their writings. For it is notorious that men of letters have generally been lacking in that worldly wisdom which amasses wealth, and have frequently been obliged to submit to the most galling humiliations to receive the means of subsistence. " I saw so many men of letters poor and despised," says the wise Voltaire, " that I made up my mind that I would not add to their number ;" and I am inclined to think the wise Shakespeare made the same resolution.

What man of any culture has not his moments of luminous thought, of rare conceptions and bright imaginings, when conversation flows like water, and the world seems lit up with celestial light? These are not the moments for ordinary acquaintance; but for that genial, intimate fellowship, when noble souls commune with each other, and appreciation kindles inspiration. Then the man exhibits himself, his soul, his nature; and it is in such moments that he does his best literary work, and incarnates his thoughts in a work of art. For a man in his best mood is as different from himself in his ordinary mood as steel is different from iron. I once heard a gentleman say, concerning an author whose writings he greatly admired, that he did not care to make his personal acquaintance, for he was sure this would simply disenchant him: "A man of genius," said he, "is seldom equal to himself in his best literary work, and his conversation would therefore fall so far short of his writings, that I should be sure to be disenchanted." "If you have a hero," says George Eliot, "do not make a journey to visit him."

This, however, is not always the case.

Some men of genius are greater in their conversation than in their printed works. This was the case with Dr. Johnson and with the poet Burns. The former lives now almost solely in Boswell's account of his talk, and Burns is reported, by those who knew him, as far more brilliant in his conversation than in his poetry. One noble lady declared that Burns was the only man whose talk took her completely off her feet. From the few notices that have come down to us of Shakespeare, we judge he must have been such a man; fully as delightful in his conversation as in his writings, delighting those who talked with him as much as those who read him. The lines which first suggested this essay may enable us to form some idea of its brilliancy. Probably his conversation has never been surpassed by that of any man who talked with his friends. Wit and brilliancy of talent were so common in his day, that the conversation even of Shakespeare was not noted as anything extraordinary. Yet he is reported by several to have been excellent company, "with a very ready and pleasant, smooth wit;" and there is little doubt that he was the head and front of that brilliant company who used to assemble at the Mermaid Tavern, whose meetings are so strikingly described by Francis Beaumont, the common friend of both Jonson and Shakespeare:

"What things have we seen
Done at the Mermaid! heard words that have been
So nimble and so full of subtle flame,
As if that every one from whom they came
Had meant to put his whole wit in a jest,
And had resolved to live a fool the rest
Of his dull life. There, where there hath been thrown
Wit and mirth enough to justify the town
For three days past; wit, that might warrant be
For the whole city to talk foolishly
Till that were cancelled; and, when that was gone,
We left an air behind us which alone
Was able to make the next two companies
Right witty."

Now let the reader glance for a moment, once again, at the Archbishop's account of the Prince's talk, and judge whether it is not that of Shakespeare himself :

> Hear him but reason in divinity,
> And, all-admiring, with an inward wish,
> You would desire the king were made a prelate:
> Hear him debate of commonwealth affairs,
> You would say, it hath been all-in-all his study :
> List his discourse of war, and you shall hear
> A fearful battle rendered you in music :
> Turn him to any course of policy,
> The Gordian knot of it he will unloose,
> Familiar as his garter; that, when he speaks,
> The air, a chartered libertine, is still,
> And the mute wonder lurketh in men's ears
> To steal his sweet and honeyed sentences.

Fuller, who was almost a contemporary of Shakespeare (born like Milton, in 1608, eight years before Shakespeare's death), makes an interesting reference to these Mermaid conferences, at which Sir Walter Raleigh is said to have been one of the participants : " Many were the wit-combats between Shakespeare and Ben Jonson, which two I behold like a Spanish great galleon and an English man-of-war. Master Jonson, like the former, was built far higher in learning; solid,

but slow in his performances. Shakespeare, like the English man-of-war, lesser
in bulk but lighter in sailing, could turn
with all tides, tack about, and take advantage of all winds by the quickness of
his wit and invention." Could there be
any better description of the Prince's
encounters with Falstaff? Was not the
Prince the light English man-of-war as
compared with the Spanish great galleon
Falstaff? Of course, Falstaff is made
the wittier of the two; but the wit of
both is the product of one brain, and the
exigencies of the drama required that the
fat knight should be made droller and
more amusing than the Prince; for he
had to "bring the house down" oftener
than the Prince, whose dignity would be
compromised by too much of this sort of
thing. The latter, however, held his
own throughout, and was always a foeman worthy of his steel.

If any one, therefore, wishes to enjoy
Shakespeare's conversations, to taste what
they were like, he must not seek them in
his biography, nor in the biographies of

9

Ben Jonson or Beaumont and Fletcher;
he must not seek them in any of the memoirs of his time; for in none of these
are they to be found;—no, he must
seek them in his writings; in the First
and Second Part of *Henry IV.* he will
find them in all their freshness. The
Poet is there, with all his spirit, life, wit
and philosophy; Ben Jonson is there,
with all his sense, humor, and raillery;
Southampton, Pembroke, and the wise
counsellors of the reign of Elizabeth are
there, with all their wise and dignified
speeches; the hostess and divers of the
frequenters of the Mermaid Tavern are
there, with all their quips, cranks and
quiddities. Nor is it in the pages of the
historians, Hume, Lingard, or Macaulay,
that he will find the personal character
and conversation of the rulers of that
day; but in the living pages of Shakespeare, which present not only the spirit,
but the flesh and blood of the men of
the time; their life and conversation in
those moments when they displayed their

inward selves, and showed what they really were.

There were no reporters, diarists, interviewers in Shakespeare's time; and very few thought it worth while to put down in black and white anything but great political events and the movements of royal personages. The art of familiar correspondence was unknown. In fact, the composition of a letter was, at that time, about as formal and deliberate a piece of business as writing a contract is to-day; for there was not merely the writing of the letter, but the folding, sealing, addressing, and transmitting, which were all much more difficult than they are at the present time, requiring taste, training and means possessed by few. This is why there are so few letters extant from that day, and why we know so little of the private lives of the great men of the time.

When the great dramas of Shakespeare were coming out, hardly anybody thought it worth while to make any written mention of them; hardly a soul spoke of them in a letter to a friend. Now the production of a new play or an opera is telegraphed over the world; the correspondent of every newspaper gives an account of it; and the whole history of its author is set down the next day in the newspapers. Not only do we learn all about the play or the opera, but the habits of its author; what he eats, drinks, and wears; who are his friends; what he says, and what books he reads. In Shakespeare's day, a man could be eminent in his profession without being made a show of. Men whose deeds have since been trumpeted over the world lived and died without any impertinent inquiries being made into their private lives. Greatness was so common that nobody thought it worth while to note with pen and ink the doings and sayings of " a mere player;" and he was too great a man to do it himself. He was not of the memoir-writing kind; nor did any of his friends think him of sufficient impor- tance to write a memoir of him, or even to make any inquiry into his life. Fame

he seems to have regarded with absolute indifference; for even his best works
might have perished for all the care he
took of them.   The last infirmity of noble
minds was not his.   We are not sure that
a single play of his was published with
his consent in his lifetime.   What was
Hecuba to him, or he to Hecuba?   He
knew that, after his death, even if the
whole world talked of him, he would
probably be as unconscious of it as the
stone that rested on his grave.*   .

As Victor Hugo observes, he came near
meeting the fate of Æschylus, whose
works were burned in the Alexandrian
Library.   "Shakespeare also had his
conflagration," says Hugo.   "He was so

---

* This extreme modesty of Shakespeare is the basis of one
of the charges against him; for Mr. Donnelly maintains, I
believe, that he never claimed the plays as his at all.   What!
did all the various quarto editions of his plays, published under his name in his lifetime, and never questioned as other
than his, nor ever disowned by him, form no claim?   How is
an author's claim then to be made out?   Did the united testimony of his contemporaries, and of all subsequent genera-
tions, form no claim?   If so, then no man may lay claim to
anything that he possesses, literary or otherwise, except it be
duly registered and filed under his name, with affidavits and
vouchers, as his personal property.

little printed, printing existing so little for him, thanks to the stupid indifference of his immediate posterity, that in 1666 there was still but one edition of the poet of Stratford-on-Avon (Hemynge and Condell's edition), three hundred copies of which were printed. Shakespeare, with this obscure and pitiful edition awaiting the public in vain, was a sort of poor but proud relative of the glorious poets. These three hundred copies were nearly all stored up in London when the Fire of 1666 broke out. It burned London, and nearly burned Shakespeare. The whole edition of Hemynge and Condell disappeared, with the exception of the forty-eight copies which had been sold in fifty years. Those forty-eight purchasers saved the works of Shakespeare!"

Forty-eight copies in fifty years! O disheartened and despondent poet! how canst thou grumble when the immortal Shakespeare was so little appreciated! Poetry is food for the gods, of whom there are few in any country. To Hemynge and Condell, who saved Shakespeare from the fate of Æschylus, and who have been so roughly and unthankfully treated by some critics, statues will yet be erected.

Victor Hugo is, however, as he often is when speaking of English affairs, not exactly correct in his statement of facts; for there were two other editions printed before 1666, one in 1632 and another in 1663; but his inferences are practically correct nevertheless. But for Hemynge and Condell's First Folio, we should, according to Halliwell-Phillipps, never have heard of such masterpieces as the *Tempest, Macbeth, Twelfth Night, Measure for Measure, Coriolanus, Julius Cæsar, Timon of Athens, Antony and Cleopatra, Cymbeline, As You Like It,* and *Winter's Tale.* How easily might these plays have been burnt! and how much we are indebted to these two friends and fellow-actors of Shakespeare for preserving them by print! O Gutenberg! how much we owe to thee for thy divine invention, the art preservative of arts, the savior of the works of genius! Print paralyzes the arm of the tyrant, and renders the works of genius indestructible. Nevermore shall a Nero or an Omar have any power over such works; nevermore shall genius be either the suppliant or the victim of potentates and princes. Print puts them beyond the power of any human being to destroy them.*

And now, because the details of his life are wanting, because we do not know the names of his teachers, the cut of his clothes, the color of his eyes, the price of his dinner, or the amount of his salary, the triflers and cranks, the gadders after personalities and novelties, the seekers after signs and wonders, the worshippers of rank and classic culture, the people who are too dull to see the man in his writings, and who cannot conceive of a man being cultivated and refined without

---

* Curiously enough, of these three hundred copies of the First Folio, thirteen are, according to Mr. Fleming, in the possession of New Yorkers, which speaks volumes for the taste and appreciation of the Empire City. See *Shakespeariana* for March, 1888.

university polish, are trying to rob him of his fair name and fame, and to add both to those of another, already full of honors for work of an entirely different kind, and famous as lawyer, legislator, philosopher, and essayist !

> " For now the Poet cannot die
>   Nor leave his music as of old ;
>   But round him ere he scarce be cold
> Begins the scandal and the cry :
>
> " ' Proclaim the faults he would not show :
>   Break lock and seal : betray the trust :
>   Keep nothing sacred ; 'tis but just
> The many-headed Beast should know !'
>
> " Ah, shameless ! for he did but sing
>   A song that pleased us from its worth ;
>   No public life was his on earth ;
> No blazoned statesman he, nor king.
>
> " He gave the people of his best ;
>   His worst he kept ; his best he gave,
>   My Shakespeare's curse on clown and knave
> Who will not let his ashes rest !"

It is worthy of notice, that the really great men of literature, those who appreciated Shakespeare most highly and criticised his works most ably, never for

a moment questioned his right to what
went under his name, never once imagined
that because he was little noticed and less
written about in his day, he was not the
author of the immortal dramas. If any
man knew the advantages of a classic
education, surely that man was Coleridge.
With what scorn he would have regarded
the attempt to foist the works of Shakespeare on Lord Bacon! Not only Coleridge, but Hazlitt, Goethe, Gervinus, and
the rest would have regarded it with
derision. As for. Miss Delia Bacon's
book on Shakespeare,—the book that first
started the whole foolish controversy,—
it is simply learning gone mad, the most
far-fetched and cranky thing ever penned.
Buzfuz's "chops and tomato-sauce" is
nothing to it; Swift's plan for extracting sunbeams from cucumbers is sensible
compared with it; Macpherson's claims
for Ossian are reasonable and probable
compared with it. Nothing out of Bed-
lam can equal the astounding deductions
she makes from his plays. The most
crazy religious enthusiast never inter-

preted passages in the Scriptures in a more extraordinary manner than Miss Delia Bacon interpreted passages in Bacon's works and Shakespeare's plays.*

---

* I did not know, when I wrote this, that this unhappy lady, Miss Delia Bacon, ended her career in an insane asylum. Had I been aware of this fact, I should not, perhaps, have used such strong language. Some Baconians assert, that the severe criticisms on her book, and the ridicule heaped upon her by all classes, were the cause of her malady; but the truth is, judging from her work, she must have been predisposed to insanity; for I never, in my whole life, read a book that looked so little like anything reasonable or sensible.

CHAPTER X.

THE KNOWN TRAITS OF SHAKESPEARE COMPARED WITH THOSE OF THE PRINCE.

THOUGH the Prince's character may be seen in almost every scene of the play, its real dignity and inner beauty come out more strongly in the interviews between himself and his father than in any other. Here he shows himself in his true colors as an honest, loving son, a faithful subject, and a patriotic prince. "Frank, liberal, prudent, gentle, yet brave as Hotspur himself," says Mr. Knight, "the Prince shows that even in his wildest excesses he has drunk deeply of the fountains of truth and wisdom. The wisdom of the king is that of a cold and subtle politician ;—Hotspur seems to stand out from his followers as the haughty feudal lord, too proud to have listened to any teacher but his own will; —but the Prince, in casting away the dignity of his station to commune freely with his fellow-men, has attained that strength which is above all conventional power; his virtues as well as his frailties belong to our common humanity; the virtues capable, therefore, of the highest elevation, and the frailties not pampered into crimes by the artificial incentives of social position."

Although he is a soldier, and brave as brave can be, he is represented as loving peace and hating bloodshed: "I am not yet of Percy's mind, the Hotspur of the North," he says; " he that kills me some six or seven dozen Scots at a breakfast, washes his hands, and says to his wife, 'Fie upon this quiet life! I want work.'" Oh no; he prefers intellectual combats to physical ones, the play of spiritual weapons to material ones; he prefers wine, wit, and wisdom to the clash of arms and the roar of cannon; genial, social intercourse, with witty sallies and lively repartees, to the mustering of troops and

the din of battle. Is not this the Shakespeare described by his contemporaries?
Is not this the Shakespeare that we know
from all accounts? Even when he becomes king, and is urged by the lords
spiritual to make war on France, see with
what anxiety he counts the cost, with
what solicitude he looks to the miseries
it will entail :

We charge you, in the name of God, take heed ;
For never two such kingdoms did contend
Without much fall of blood ; whose guiltless drops
Are every one a woe, a sore complaint,
'Gainst him whose wrongs give edge unto the swords
That make such waste in brief mortality.

"Brief mortality," indeed! he felt that
life was all too short without having
it curtailed by violence. His hatred of
bloodshed was exhibited, indeed, long
before he became king. To prevent the
fratricidal slaughter of his countrymen in
battle, he thus offers to fight in single
combat the most renowned warrior of his
day :

Prince. In both our armies there is many a soul
Shall pay full dearly for this encounter,

If once they join in trial.   Tell your nephew
The prince of Wales doth join with all the world
In praise of Henry Percy.   By my hopes,
This present enterprise set off his head,
I do not think a braver gentleman,
More active-valiant, or more valiant-young,
More daring, or more bold, is now alive
To grace this latter age with noble deeds.
For my part, I may speak it to my shame,
I have a truant been to chivalry,
And so I hear he doth account me too ;
Yet this before my father's majesty :
I am content, that he shall take the odds
Of his great name and estimation,
And will, to save the blood on either side,
Try fortune with him in a single fight.

And when Hotspur, hearing of the challenge, asks,

How showed his tasking ? seemed it in contempt ?

Sir Richard Vernon replies thus beautifully :

No, by my soul : I never in my life
Did hear a challenge urged more modestly,
Unless a brother should a brother dare
To gentle exercise and proof of arms.
He gave you all the duties of a man,
Trimmed up your praises with a princely tongue,
Spoke your deservings like a chronicle,

Making you ever better than his praise,
By still dispraising praise, valued with you ;
And, which became him like a prince indeed,
He made a blushing cital of himself ;
And chid his truant youth with such a grace,
As if he mastered there a double spirit,
Of teaching, and of learning, instantly.
There did he pause : but let me tell the world,
If he outlive the envy of this day,
England did never owe so sweet a hope,
So much misconstrued in his wantonness.

The modesty of Shakespeare is proverbial ; he never speaks of himself directly ; he never advances any views that we know to be his own individually ; all these things are foreign to his nature. But here, in disguise, he freely and truly paints himself, justly imagining the Prince to be such a man as he was, and justly and without any other desire than painting a true character, following the highest instincts of his nature. Consider, therefore, how near these lines touch him :

He made a blushing cital of himself ;
And chid his truant youth with such a grace,
As if he mastered there a double spirit,
Of teaching, and of learning, instantly.

" A blushing cital of himself," and " a double spirit of teaching and of learning !" Could anything be more like the Poet ? Is it not largely on account of his modest nature that we know so little of him ? Can we not conceive that his conversation was of this *teaching* and *learning* character ? Who ever learned and who ever taught as he did ? His talks with his friends and companions would surely have been of such a character. And then how true to the letter did he make these lines :

> Let me tell the world,
> If he outlive the envy of this day,
> England did never owe so sweet a hope,
> So much misconstrued in his wantonness.

To partake in an encounter of wits, to cross intellectual swords with a foeman worthy of his steel, the Prince was willing to go extraordinary lengths ; and who will deny that Shakespeare, to enjoy an uncommon intellectual treat, would be willing to have a tête-à-tête with the devil himself ? Hence the extraordinary companions the Prince draws around him ; hence the extraordinary situations

10

he gets into for a prince. When he resolves to appear before Falstaff and his mistress as a drawer or pot-boy, he exclaims: " From a prince to a 'prentice! a low transformation! That shall be mine; for in everything *the purpose must weigh with the folly!* " Witness his extraordinary delight at the wit of Falstaff's page, and his immediate reward of him therefor:

Poins. . . . . . By the mass, here comes Bardolph.

Prince. And the boy that I gave Falstaff: he had him from me Christian; and look, if the fat villain have not transformed him ape!

Enter BARDOLPH *and Page.*

Bard. God save your grace!

Prince. And yours, most noble Bardolph.

Bard. [*To the Page.*] Come, you virtuous ass, you bashful fool, must you be blushing? wherefore blush you now?

Page. He called me even now, my lord, through a red lattice, and I could discern no part of his face from the window; at last I spied his eyes; and methought he had made two holes in the ale-wife's new red petticoat, and peeped through!

Prince. Hath not the boy profited?

Bard. Away, you upright rabbit, away!

Page. Away, you rascally Althea's dream, away!

Prince. Instruct us, boy; what dream, boy?

Page. Marry, my lord, Althea dreamt she was delivered of a firebrand; and therefore I call him her dream. [*Bardolph had a very red nose.*]

Prince. A crown's worth of good interpretation. —There it is, boy. [*Gives him money.*

Poins. O, that this good blossom could be kept from cankers!—Well, there is sixpence to preserve thee.

Would not Shakespeare be just the man to reward the witty gamin for a stroke of this kind?

There is one other sentence of the Prince's, uttered just before the merry meeting, and after his practical joke with Francis, which has always seemed to me marvellously significant. Most writers, when they will give a picture of the poet, quote the famous lines:

The poet's eye in a fine frenzy rolling,
Doth glance from heaven to earth, from earth to
    heaven : etc.

But, to my thinking, these words addressed by the Prince to Poins give a far truer picture of such a character : " I am now of all humors, that have showed themselves humors, since the old days of goodman Adam, to the pupil age of this present twelve o'clock at midnight."

Of all humors! Truly, the very picture of poets. Of how many poets do we not know this to have been precisely the character? Is not the history of Coleridge, Byron, Shelley, Burns, Poe, and the rest a history of men " of all humors," "of jars all compact," guilty of such extravagant freaks that men of common-sense have usually set them down as uncanny? Sometimes guilty of the most fantastic tricks and wild extravagances; sometimes down in the deepest depths of melancholy; sometimes up in the highest heights of heaven; sometimes all that is holy and devout; sometimes all that is wicked and devilish,—they go beyond the bounds observed by other men. Turn to the history of almost any of our modern English poets, and you shall find them to have been " of all humors, that have showed themselves humors, since the old days of goodman Adam." And Shakespeare, though wise and prudent beyond most poets, was not different from them in this respect. We know that he had his humors, his freaks, his practical jokes, his wild youthful escapades, and that his very death was caused by a merry meeting among old friends and fellow-poets. Yet he is known for such gentleness of disposition and such kindness of manner that Matthew Arnold's description of Shelley's character might stand for that of our Poet : "A man of marvellous gentleness, of feminine refinement, with gracious and considerate manner, 'a perfect gentleman,' entirely without arrogance or aggressive egotism, completely devoid of the proverbial and ferocious vanity of authors and poets, always disposed to make little of his own work and to prefer that of others, of reverent enthusiasm for the great and wise, of high and tender seriousness, of heroic generosity, and of a delicacy in rendering services which was equal to his generosity." Who will say that these words might not be applied to the great dramatist, or to his image, the Prince?

But the Prince was a soldier. Well, so were many eminent poets and philosophers; so were Æschylus, Socrates, Cervantes, and Ben Jonson;—and I have not a doubt that Shakespeare could, had he been so minded, have distinguished himself in the field as he did elsewhere; for, like these his great predecessors and contemporaries, he was as heroic in character as he was noble and grand in thought. Although philosopher enough to "daff the world aside and bid it pass," he could, when required, have matched with the bravest or the ablest in the field. If we follow the Prince through his campaigns as king, we find high thoughts and brave actions going hand in hand; and had the Poet been actually king, we may be sure the one would have accompanied the other as the night the day. What actual king ever thought so highly, spoke so eloquently, acted so nobly, or fought so heroically as did Shakespeare's Henry the Fifth? Consider for a mo-

ment one of his speeches to his army,
and tell me if the man Shakespeare
might not have spoken thus:

Once more unto the breach, dear friends, once
    more;
Or close the wall up with our English dead!
In peace, there's nothing so becomes a man,
As modest stillness and humility;
But when the blast of war blows in our ears,
Then imitate the action of the tiger:
Stiffen the sinews, summon up the blood,
Disguise fair nature with hard-favored rage:
Then lend the eye a terrible aspect;
Let it pry through the portage of the head,
Like the brass cannon; let the brow o'erwhelm it
As fearfully as doth a galled rock
O'erhang and jutty his confounded base,
Swilled with the wild and wasteful ocean.
Now set the teeth, and stretch the nostril wide;
Hold hard the breath, and bend up every spirit
To his full height!—On, on, you noblest English!
Whose blood is fetched from fathers of war-proof!
Fathers, that, like so many Alexanders,
Have in these parts from morn till even fought,
And sheathed their swords for lack of argument.
Dishonor not your mothers: now attest,
That those whom you called fathers did beget you.
Be copy now to men of grosser blood,
And teach them how to war.—And you, good yeo-
    men,

Whose limbs were made in England, show us here
The mettle of your pasture : let us swear
That you are worth your breeding ; which I doubt
    not,
For there is none of you so mean and base,
That hath not noble luster in your eyes.
I see you stand like greyhounds in the slips,
Straining upon the start. The game's afoot :
Follow your spirit ; and, upon this charge,
Cry—God for Harry ! England ! and St. George !

Although a good soldier and brave man, the Prince had, however, like the man whom he represented, far too merciful a disposition and compassionate a heart for a soldier of his day. No soldier of that day, nor hardly any of this, would ever have addressed the inhabitants of a city, which he was about to assault and plunder, as this soldier addressed the inhabitants of Harfleur. When Blücher first saw London, after the battle of Waterloo, his natural exclamation was, " What a city to plunder ! " Compare this with King Henry's address to the Harfleurians. See how fearfully conscious he is of the horrors of war !

Before the Gates of Harfleur.

The Governor and some Citizens on the Walls; the English Forces below. Enter King HENRY *and his Train.*

K. Hen.   How yet resolves the governor of the town?
This is the latest parle we will admit:
Therefore, to our best mercy give yourselves,
Or, like to men proud of destruction,
Defy us to our worst: for, as I am a soldier,
(A name that, in my thoughts, becomes me best,)
If I begin the battery once again,
I will not leave the half-achieved Harfleur,
Till in her ashes she lie buried.
The gates of mercy shall be all shut up;
And the flesh'd soldier, rough and hard of heart,
In liberty of bloody hand, shall range
With conscience wide as hell; mowing like grass
Your fresh fair virgins, and your flowering infants.
What is it then to me, if impious war,
Array'd in flames, like to the prince of fiends,
Do, with his smirch'd complexion, all fell feats
Enlink to waste and desolation?
What is't to me, when you yourselves are cause,
If your pure maidens fall into the hand
Of hot and forcing violation?
What rein can hold licentious wickedness,
When down the hill he holds his fierce career?
We may as bootless spend our vain command
Upon the enraged soldiers in their spoil,
As send precepts to the Leviathan

To come ashore. Therefore, you men of Harfleur,
Take pity of your town, and of your people,
Whiles yet my soldiers are in my command ;
Whiles yet the cool and temperate wind of grace
O'erblows the filthy and contagious clouds
Of deadly murder, spoil, and villany.
If not, why, in a moment, look to see
The blind and bloody soldier with foul hand
Defile the locks of your shrill-shrieking daughters ;
Your fathers taken by the silver beards,
And their most reverend heads dashed to the walls ;
Your naked infants spitted upon pikes ;
Whiles the mad mothers with their howls confus'd
Do break the clouds, as did the wives of Jewry
At Herod's bloody-hunting slaughtermen.
What say you ? will you yield, and this avoid ?
Or, guilty in defence, be thus destroy'd ?
    Gov. Our expectation hath this day an end :
The dauphin, whom of succor we entreated,
Returns us—that his powers are not yet ready
To raise so great a siege. Therefore, dread king,
We yield our town, and lives, to thy soft mercy :
Enter our gates ; dispose of us, and ours ;
For we no longer are defensible.
    K. Hen. Open your gates.—Come uncle Exeter,
Go you and enter Harfleur ; there remain,
And fortify it strongly 'gainst the French :
Use mercy to them all.

This was not a man who, like the
Spanish generals in the Netherlands,

could make terms of surrender with the inhabitants of a city, and then give them up to indiscriminate slaughter. Not only does he see and anxiously apprehend all the horrors of the assaulting and plundering of the city, but he feels profound pity on the inhabitants at the dread prospect, and eloquently beseeches them to have pity on themselves!

But I wished to draw the reader's attention to the Prince's character as displayed in his interviews with his father. Bolingbroke was a politician ; Mr. Knight calls him "a cold, subtle politician ;" he was, nevertheless, according to Shakespeare, a wise and thoughtful man. John Shakespeare, the father of the Poet, was also a politician in his way, and a man of no mean character ; for he gradually fought his way up, from various subordinate and inferior positions, to be chief magistrate of his native town, and was a man of more than common force of character. The bare fact that he held all the various offices which he filled without any knowledge of letters is proof positive that the man, was a ruler of men by right of nature, by divine right : he won his position by sheer superiority of character. Although he could not write his own name, he dominated over all those in Stratford that could ; he was their leading and foremost man in all important affairs : the patron and friend of actors and artists ; the man who came forward to receive the great ones of the earth (including perhaps Queen Elizabeth herself) when such came officially to the town, and the man who patriotically guarded its interests. For his office of chamberlain of the borough is described as one of great responsibility, and that of bailiff or mayor as the highest honor that the corporation could bestow ; so that he was literally "a king of men" among those over whom he ruled.

The circumstance (shown by all his biographers) that Shakespeare helped his father with his very first earnings in London, is also an interesting and significant fact ; it displays a dutiful and loving son, and infers a worthy father; and when we remember that the Prince breaks Falstaff's head for "likening his father to a singing man of Windsor;" that he tells Poins "his heart bleeds inwardly that his father is so sick," and that Shakespeare loyally stood by his father and actually obtained papers from the herald's office to make him legally a gentleman, we cannot but infer that these facts hold together and coincide. Do not these things show that he honored his father and stood by him in trouble? and did not the Prince do the same?

We may be sure, from the fact that John Shakespeare was considered worthy of receiving in marriage the hand of a woman of birth and fortune, a woman belonging to one of the most ancient and honorable families in Warwickshire, that he was known and respected as a man of superior character, of innate worth and respectability, among all his neighbors. His wife, whose maiden name was Mary Arden, was the daughter of Robert Arden of Wilmecote, a gentleman of good

landed estate, and descendant of Sir
John Arden, squire of the body of Henry
VII. "Mary Arden," says Mr. T. Spencer Baynes, in his admirable account of
Shakespeare in the "Encyclopædia Britannica," "was a gentlewoman in the
truest sense of the term, and she would
bring into her husband's household elements of character and culture that
would be of priceless value to the family,
and especially to the eldest son, who naturally had the first place in her care and
love. A good mother is to an imaginative boy his earliest ideal of womanhood,
and in her, for him, are gathered up, in all
their vital fulness, the tenderness, sympathy, and truth, the infinite love, patient
watchfulness, and self-abnegation of the
whole sex. And the experience of his
mother's bearing and example during the
vicissitudes of their home-life must have
been for the future dramatist a vivid revelation of the more sprightly and gracious, as well as of the profounder elements, of female character. In the earlier and prosperous days at Stratford,

when all within the home-circle was bright and happy, and in her intercourse with her boy, Mary Shakespeare could freely unfold the attractive qualities that had so endeared her to her father's heart ; the delightful image of the young mother would melt unconsciously in the boy's mind, fill his imagination, and become a storehouse whence in after years he would draw some of the finest lines in his matchless portraiture of women."

Now, then, being so fathered and so mothered, might not Shakespeare, when composing the scenes between the Prince and his father, have in mind something of the manner and language which his own father used in reasoning with him on his early excesses and imprudences ? Might he not have still fresh in mind how he too violated the law, of which his father was a pillar, and on account of which his father's reprimands must have been all the more severe ? And might not some tinge of this recollection be the originator and prompter of these remarkably interesting, touching and instructive scenes between the Prince and his father? So that the reader will perceive that these scenes are still in keeping with my view that the Poet depicted himself in the Prince, and that he still drew from personal experiences in writing these passages. Let the reader turn to the Fourth Scene in the Fourth Act of the Second Part of *Henry the Fourth*,—too long to be inserted here,—and judge for himself; let him read these passages carefully, and he will perceive that they are simply the natural conferences of father and son, drawn by the hand and colored by the imagination of a poet.

CHAPTER XI.

SCENE WITH THE CHIEF JUSTICE—THE PRINCE CONTRASTED WITH HIS BROTHER JOHN—TESTIMONY OF THE POET'S CONTEMPORARIES AS TO HIS GENTLE CHARACTER.

AFTER perusing this scene, and noting especially the lines,

> If I do feign,
> O! let me in my present wildness die,
> And never live to show the incredulous world
> The noble change that I have purposed,

the reader will be ready for the scene in which the king's best hopes are realized, and the noble and magnanimous behavior of his son toward the Chief Justice is shown: a scene so beautiful, so full of noble lines, and exhibiting the Prince in so amiable a light,—acting and speaking as we cannot help thinking the Poet

11

would have acted and spoken in his
place,—that I cannot forbear giving it
entire, without omitting a single word.

SCENE II.—Westminster.   A Room in the Palace.
Enter WARWICK, *and the Lord Chief Justice.*

War.   How now, my lord chief justice? whither
  away?

Ch. Just.   How doth the king?

War.   Exceeding well; his cares are now all
  ended.

Ch. Just.   I hope, not dead?

War.   He's walk'd the way of nature.
And to our purposes, he lives no more.

Ch. Just.   I would his majesty had called me with
  him :
The service that I truly did his life
Hath left me open to all injuries.

War.   Indeed, I think the young king loves you
  not.

Ch. Just.   I know he doth not ; and do arm my-
  self,
To welcome the condition of the time ;
Which cannot look more hideously upon me
Than I have drawn it in my fantasy.

Enter Prince JOHN, *Prince* HUMPHREY, CLARENCE,
  WESTMORELAND, *and others.*

War.   Here comes the heavy issue of dead Harry :
O, that the living Harry had the temper
Of him, the worst of these three gentlemen !

How many nobles then should hold their places,
That must strike sail to spirits of vile sort!
 Ch. Just. Alas! I fear, all will be overturn'd.
 P. John. Good-morrow, cousin Warwick.
 P. Humph. Good-morrow, cousin.
 P. John. We meet like men that had forgot to
   speak.
 War. We do remember; but our argument
Is all too heavy to admit much talk.
 P. John. Well, peace be with him that hath made
   us heavy!
 Ch. Just. Peace be with us, least we be heavier!
 P. Humph. O; good my lord, you have lost a
   friend indeed:
And I dare swear, you borrow not that face
Of seeming sorrow; it is, sure, your own.
 P. John. Though no man be assur'd what grace
   to find,
You stand in coldest expectation:
I am the sorrier; would 'twere otherwise.
 Cla. Well, you must now speak Sir John Falstaff
   fair;
Which swims against your stream of quality.
 Ch. Just. Sweet princes, what I did, I did in
   honor,
Led by the impartial conduct of my soul;
And never shall you see, that I will beg
A ragged and forestall'd remission.—
If truth and upright innocency fail me,
I'll to the king my master that is dead,
And tell him who hath sent me after him.

War.   Here comes the prince.

Enter Prince HENRY, *as* KING.

Ch. Just.   Good-morrow; and heaven save your
    majesty!

King.   This new and gorgeous garment, majesty,
Sits not so easy on me as you think.—
Brothers, you mix your sadness with some fear:
This is the English, not the Turkish court;
Not Amurath an Amurath succeeds,
But Harry, Harry.   Yet be sad, good brothers,
For, to speak truth, it very well becomes you:
Sorrow so royally in you appears,
That I will deeply put the fashion on,
And wear it in my heart.   Why, then, be sad:
But entertain no more of it, good brothers,
Than a joint burden laid upon us all.
For me, by Heaven, I bid you be assured,
I'll be your father and your brother too;
Let me but bear your love, I'll bear your cares.
Yet weep that Harry's dead; and so will I:
But Harry lives, that shall convert those tears,
By number, into hours of happiness.

   P. John, etc.   We hope no other from your majesty.

   King.   You all look strangely on me:—and you
    most: [*To the Chief Justice.*
You are, I think, assured, I love you not.

   Ch. Just.   I am assured, if I be measured rightly,
Your majesty hath no just cause to hate me.

   King.   No!
How might a prince of my great hopes forget
So great indignities you laid upon me?

What ! rate, rebuke, and roughly send to prison
The immediate heir of England ! Was this easy?
May this be washed in Lethe and forgotten ?
   Ch. Just. I then did use the person of your
           father ;
The image of his power lay then in me :
And, in the administration of his law,
Whiles I was busy for the commonwealth,
Your highness pleased to forget my place,
The majesty and power of law and justice,
The image of the king whom I presented,
And struck me in my very seat of judgment :
Whereon, as an offender to your father,
I gave bold way to my authority,
And did commit you.   If the deed were ill,
Be you contented, wearing now the garland,
To have a son set your decrees at nought ;
To pluck down justice from your awful bench ;
To trip the course of law, and blunt the sword
That guards the peace and safety of your person :
Nay, more : to spurn at your most royal image,
And mock your workings in a second body.
Question your royal thoughts, make the case yours ;
Be now the father, and propose a son :
Hear your own dignity so much profaned,
See your most dreadful laws so loosely slighted,
Behold yourself so by a son disdained :
And then imagine me taking your part,
And, in your power, soft silencing your son :
After this cold consideration, sentence me ;
And, as you are a king, speak in your state,

What I have done that misbecame my place,
My person, or my liege's sovereignty.
   King. You are right, justice, and you weigh
       this well ;
Therefore still bear the balance and the sword :
And I do wish your honors may increase,
Till you do live to see a son of mine
Offend you, and obey you, as I did.
So shall I live to speak my father's words :—
" Happy am I, that have a man so bold,
That dares do justice on my proper son ;
And not less happy, having such a son,
That would deliver up his greatness so
Into the hands of justice."—You did commit me :
For which I do commit into your hand
The unstained sword that you have used to bear :
With this remembrance,—That you use the same
With the like bold, just, and impartial spirit,
As you have done 'gainst me. There is my hand ;
You shall be as a father to my youth :
My voice shall sound as you do prompt mine ear ;
And I will stoop and humble my intents
To your well-practised, wise directions.—
And, princes all, believe me, I beseech you :
My father is gone wild into his grave,
For in his tomb lie my affections ;
And with his spirit sadly I survive,
To mock the expectation of the world ;
To frustrate prophecies ; and to raze out
Rotten opinion, who hath writ me down
After my seeming. The tide of blood in me

Hath proudly flowed in vanity till now;
Now doth it turn, and ebb back to the sea :
Where it shall mingle with the state of floods,
And flow henceforth in formal majesty.
Now call we our high court of parliament :
And let us choose such limbs of noble counsel,
That the great body of our state may go
In equal rank with the best governed nation ;
That war, or peace, or both at once, may be
As things acquainted and familiar to us ;—
In which you, father, shall have foremost hand.

                [*To the Lord Chief Justice.*

Our coronation done, we will accite,
As I before remembered, all our state :
And (God consigning to my good intents)
No prince, nor peer, shall have just cause to say,
Heaven shorten Harry's happy life one day !

What a contrast is all this to the wretched conduct of his brother John ! What a contrast does the Prince's treatment of the Chief Justice present to John's mean and infamous behavior in delivering up the surrendered noblemen to the hangman ! If the Prince were made to commit any atrocity of this kind, I should say at once, " No; this cannot be the Poet;" but he never does; such conduct is foreign to his nature. He is always kind, considerate, merciful, and magnanimous.

When Falstaff finds that his wit has no effect upon John, that treacherous and cruel prince, he exclaims: " This same young sober-blooded boy doth not love me, and a man cannot make him laugh." Of course he cannot make him laugh ; for it needs a heart as well as a head to appreciate wit, and Prince John had neither. " He who cannot be softened into gayety," says Johnson, "cannot easily be melted into kindness."   " And none," adds Hudson, " are so hopeless as those who have no bowels."   Let the reader remember Prince Henry's kindness to the tapsters, to the page of Falstaff, to Mrs. Quickly, and to all with whom he came in contact ; let him remember that the Poet was universally esteemed for the gentleness and kindliness of his demeanor toward all with whom he had any dealings ; let him remember that when the actors had rejected Ben Jonson's play, *Every Man in his Humor*, Shakespeare took it up, found something meritorious in it, and caused it to be accepted; let him compare these actions with those of the Prince, and he will not fail to become convinced that the Prince and the Poet are one and the same person.

" Falstaff's pride of wit," says Mr. Hudson, commenting on his encounter with Prince John, "a pride which is most especially gratified in the fascination he has upon Prince Henry, is shrewdly manifested here, while at the same time a very important and operative principle of human character in general, and of Prince John's character in particular, is most hintingly touched. Falstaff sees that the brain of this sober-blooded boy has nothing for him to get hold of or work upon; that, be he ever so witty in himself, he cannot be the cause of any wit in him; and he is vexed and mortified that his wit fails upon him. And the Poet meant no doubt to have it understood that Prince Henry was drawn and held to Falstaff by virtue of something that raised him immeasurably above his brother; and that the frozen regularity which was proof against all the batteries of wit and humor was all of a piece, vitally, with the moral hardness which would not flinch from such an abominable act of perfidy as that towards the Archbishop and his party." True, Mr. Hudson, very true; he possessed "something that raised him immeasurably above his brother," who had nothing of the noble and brilliant character of the Prince, whose characteristics were all gentle and noble, like those of the Poet. How much the Prince (or the Poet) enjoyed humor, and how heartily he could laugh, we may see from what Falstaff is going to make out of Shallow: "I will devise matter enough out of this Shallow to keep Prince Harry in continual laughter the wearing out of six fashions (which is four terms or two actions), and he shall laugh without intervallums. O! you shall see him laugh, till his face be like a wet blanket ill laid up!"

With all his faults, with all his wild pranks and loose talk, there is perhaps no more essentially noble, humane, and magnanimous character in literature than this Henry, Prince of Wales, now become king, and whom we have every reason to regard as the likeness of Shakespeare. Not only do we find him showing the gentlest, kindest condescension to persons of low degree, but suing for grace, favor, and liberty to rebels and insurgents of high degree, men who endeavored to dethrone his father and ruin his family, men who, like the redoubtable Douglas, were the most formidable enemies of himself and his house:

> Go to the Douglas, and deliver him
> Up to his pleasure, ransomless, and free:
> His valor, shown upon our crests to-day,
> Hath taught us how to cherish such high deeds,
> Even in the bosom of our adversaries.

And when that prince of cowards, Falstaff, takes up Percy's body and is carrying it off as the proof of his valor, how magnanimously the Prince covers his deception!

> Come, bring your luggage nobly on your back:
> For my part, if a lie may do thee grace,
> I'll gild it with the happiest terms I have.

Might not this be regarded, not only as characteristic of the Poet's magnanimity, but of his indifference to fame?

Shortly before sailing for France, the Prince (now king) thus displays "the attribute to awe and majesty," toward an unfortunate offender of the hour:

King.   Uncle of Exeter,
Enlarge the man committed yesterday,
That railed against our person : we consider
It was excess of wine that set him on ;
And, on his more advice, we pardon him.
    Scroop.   That's mercy ; but too much security.
Let him be punished, sovereign ; lest example
Breed by this sufferance more of such a kind.
    King.   O ! let us yet be merciful.

It is true, this mercy to " the man that railed against our person yesterday " serves to make his condemnation of the bribed traitors who were about to murder him, all the more severe and unexpected ; but this is history, and the other is a stroke of character.

Before concluding this chapter, let me say a word or two more touching the character of the Prince, that I may compare it with the character of the Poet as reported by his contemporaries.

With all his extravagant and roystering ways, we feel that the Prince was, like the Poet, the quintessence of honor in his every-day life. " Do thou stand for my father," he says to Falstaff, " and examine me upon the particulars of my life." He is no more afraid to answer for the particulars of his life than to meet the most powerful enemies of his house, Douglas, Percy, and Glendower; for he knows there is as little dishonor in the one as dread in the other.

When he appears before his father, he tells him plainly he is not so bad as he is painted :

> So please your majesty, I would I could
> Quit all offences with as clear excuse,
> As well as, I am doubtless, I can purge
> Myself of many I am charged withal.

When reproached with making himself too common in the public eye, and losing his "princely privilege with vile participation," he does not say he has been bad and will reform ; but

> I shall hereafter, my thrice gracious lord,
> Be more myself.

And when his father goes so far as to say:

> Thou art like enough, through vassal fear,
> Base inclination, and the start of spleen,
> To fight against me under Percy's pay;

he exclaims:

> Do not think so; you shall not find it so!
> And God forgive them that so much have swayed
> Your majesty's good thoughts away from me.

All which answers completely to the character of the Poet; for although known to have been fond of companionship of all sorts, and to have engaged in wild pranks, he has never been accused, by any reputable person, of dishonorable or disgraceful actions.

No man is more conscious of the evil of his surroundings than the Prince. "Why, thou globe of sinful continents," he says to Falstaff, "what a life dost thou lead!" Behind the mask of revelry and laughter, we may easily perceive the earnest and thoughtful countenance of the deep-thinking man. To see how full-charged his mind and heart are, we have but to turn to his soliloquies by the death-bed of his father:

> Why doth the crown lie there upon his pillow,
> Being so troublesome a bedfellow!
> O, polished perturbation! golden care!
> That keep'st the ports of slumber open wide
> To many a watchful night!—Sleep with it now!
> Yet not so sound, and half so deeply sweet,
> As he, whose brow with homely biggin bound,
> Snores out the watch of night. O majesty!
> When thou dost pinch thy bearer, thou dost sit
> Like a rich armor worn in heat of day,
> That scalds with safety.

Could Hamlet himself have spoken more philosophically, or more eloquently? Even in the midst of his revelry, he suddenly exclaims, " Well, thus we play the fools with the time, and the spirits of the wise sit in the clouds and mock us!" And at the end of the scene in which he and Poins surprise Falstaff with his mistress, he thus takes his leave of them:

> By Heaven, Poins, I feel me much to blame
> So idly to profane the precious time,
> When tempest of commotion, like the south,

Borne with black vapor, doth begin to melt,
And drop upon our bare unarmed heads.
Give me my sword and cloak.—Falstaff, good night.

Even in that "Falstaff, good night" there shines the magnanimous soul of one who could bear no ill-will even to one who had just heaped upon him a load of unmerited abuse.

Wherever it is possible, Shakespeare makes him the mild, gentle, thoughtful man he was himself; gentle and condescending to his inferiors, nimble-witted and charming among his equals, and kind and considerate to his inferiors. From the testimony of his contemporaries, it is evident that Shakespeare was loved by all that knew him, and hated by none. "Our sweet Will," "the gentle bard of Avon," "that same gentle spirit," "our pleasant Willy," "that gentle shepherd," "honey-tongued Shakespeare," are the expressions by which he is characterized by them. "The man whom Nature's self hath made to mock herself, and truth to imitate," is Spenser's happy phrase. "Myself have seen his demeanor, no less civil than excellent in the quality he professes," is Chettle's valuable testimony. "I love the man, and do honor his memory this side idolatry," is the warm expression of his intimate friend Ben Jonson. "He was very good company, and of a very ready and pleasant smooth wit," says Aubrey. "He redeemed his vices with his virtues," says Ben Jonson, "and there was more in him to be praised than to be blamed."

Could any words characterize the Prince better than these? Did he not "redeem his vices with his virtues?" and was there not. "more in him to be praised than to be blamed?" Hudson, one of the very best of all Shakespeare's editors and biographers, thus sums up the Poet's character : " Scanty as are the materials, enough we think has been given to show that in all the common dealings of life, Shakespeare was eminently gentle, candid, upright, and judicious ; open-hearted, genial, and sweet in his social intercourse ; among his companions and

12

friends full of playful wit and sprightly grace; kind to the faults of others, severe to his own; quick to discern and acknowledge merit in another, modest and slow of finding it in himself; while in the smooth and happy marriage, which he seems to have realized, of the highest poetry and art with systematic and successful prudence in business affairs, we have an example of compact and well-rounded practical manhood, such as may justly engage our perpetual admiration." And Mr. Halliwell thus ends his account of him : " The character of Shakespeare is even better than his history. We have direct and undeniable proofs that he was prudent and active in the business of life, judicious and honest, possessing great conversational talent, universally esteemed as gentle and amiable; yet more desirous of accumulating property than of increasing his reputation, and occasionally indulging in courses irregular and wild, but not incompatible with this generic summary."

Who will say that all this has no resemblance to the Prince?   Can it not be easily conceived that the Poet's picture of the Prince is just that of himself in his youth, when he " indulged in the courses irregular and wild," so much spoken of by his biographers?   But there are other considerations, still stronger, to fortify the truth of this conception.

CHAPTER XII.

THE STAGE AS A PROFESSION IN SHAKE-
SPEARE'S TIME—THE POET'S ARRIVAL IN
LONDON, AND HIS FIRST OCCUPATION
AND COMPANIONSHIP THERE.

THE theater was, in Shakespeare's time, like the newspaper press of to-day, the one arena toward which an intellectual youth, arriving in a great city, naturally gravitated. It was the great place of recreation, toward which, as it afforded instruction as well as amusement, the people crowded in constantly increasing numbers. "It is pretty evident," says Mr. Hudson, "that in Shakespeare's time the drama was decidedly a great institution; it was a sort of Fourth Estate in the realm, nearly as much so perhaps as the newspaper press is in our day. Practically, the government of the Commonwealth was vested in king, lords, commons, and dramatists, including in the latter both writers and actors; so that the Poet had far more reason than now exists for making Hamlet say to the old statesman : 'After your death you had better have a bad epitaph, than their ill report while you live.' Perhaps we may add," says the same writer, "as illustrating the prodigious rush of life and thought towards the drama in that age, that, besides the dozen authors of whom I have spoken, Henslowe's Diary shows the names of thirty other dramatists, most of whom have propagated some part of their workmanship down to our time; and in the same document there are recorded, during the twelve years beginning in February, 1591, the titles of not fewer than 270 pieces, either as original compositions or as revivals of older plays." Stephen Gosson, in his Tract entitled " Plays confuted in Five Actions," published in 1581, has this re- markable description of the activity of the London stage at this time : " I may boldly say it, because I have seen it, that *The Palace of Pleasure, The Golden Ass, The Ethiopian History, Amadis of France, The Round Table*, and bawdy comedies in Latin, French, Italian and Spanish, have been thoroughly ransacked, to furnish the play-houses in London."

And in the *Return from Parnassus*, a poem published in 1601, there is a passage which strikingly illustrates the wonderful success and enviable position of the Players of the time, the last line in which may refer directly to Shakespeare himself :

> England affords those glorious vagabonds,
> That carried erst their fardels on their backs,
> Coursers to ride on through the gazing streets,
> Sweeping it in their glaring satin suits ;
> With mouthing words that better wits have framed,
> They purchased lands, and now esquires are made.

Here then was a market for dramatic genius ; here was an opportunity for him who could produce anything new, fresh, and original in dramatic literature ; here was the sphere, the companionship, the sights, scenes, and sounds which attracted

the youthful genius, full of all noble fancies, in love with poetry and romance,
and burning for a place among the
world's heroes. Such was the arena into
which Shakespeare entered; such was
the promising field that attracted him to
London; and such was the market in
which he grew rich. Here he found an
occupation in which he could bring all
his noble faculties into play. He wanted
scope for powers greater than those
of the money-maker; he wanted room
for the expression of his thought, his
fancies and conceptions; and the theater,
of all the places in the world, was the
one place most favorable for this purpose. Unknown and uninfluential as he
was, there was no other position so ac-
cessible to him; none other so suitable
for him. The comfortable situations
in the government service were mo-
nopolized by the nobility and gentry;
these were theirs by a sort of natural
right; and the Poet had to look for his
living in a more active situation. Thus
both fortune and his tastes pointed

the same way. Even if he could have had his choice, he would probably have preferred a position in the theater to one in the government. Be that as it may, we know that he enrolled himself in one of those dramatic companies which he subsequently styled " the abstracts and brief chronicles of the time ;" and, having once done so, he bent all his energies to master everything connected with it.

Nor did he come into unworthy company ; for the dramatic societies of that day seem to have been made up of generous and noble souls, fit associates even for Shakespeare. Davies, his contemporary, thus writes of them in 1603 :

Players, I love ye and your quality,
  As ye are men that pastime not abused;
And some I love for painting poesy,
  And say fell Fortune cannot be excused
That hath for better uses you refused :
  Wit, courage, good shape, good parts, and all
    good,
As long as all these goods are no worse used :
  And though the stage doth stain pure gentle
    blood,
Yet generous ye are in mind and mood.

This is excellent testimony to their character and quality. Who would not like to belong to a company that had "wit, courage, good shape, good parts," and were "generous in mind and mood"? Such were the men with whom Shakespeare associated; such were the characters with whom he played and for whose acting he wrote his plays.

It is exceedingly probable, from various circumstances in his family history, that Shakespeare knew something of these players before he left Stratford; for his father is known to have been friendly to the actors who visited Stratford, and I am inclined to believe that he was the personal friend of some of them. Several of those who subsequently acted with Shakespeare in London and elsewhere—notably Burbage, Green, and Tooley—were from the same county as himself, and it is probable that these townsmen of his were the personal friends of his father as well as of himself. Even if they were not, it is not likely that when there came to London the son of the former chief magistrate of Stratford, who had been the friend and patron of the players that visited the town, he would have been received with coldness or indifference. We may be sure that young Shakespeare took advantage of his father's generous hospitality toward the strolling players, not only to witness their performances, but to cultivate their personal acquaintance in Stratford.

A gentleman named Willis, born in the same year as Shakespeare, 1564, gives, in a narrative of his life, an account of "a stage-play which he saw when he was a child," which seems strongly to fortify the supposition that Shakespeare witnessed such plays in his youth. "In the city of Gloucester," says he, "the manner is, as I think it is in other like corporations, that, when players of enterludes come to towne, they first attend the Mayor to enforme him what nobleman's servants they are, and so to get licence for their publike playing ; and if the Mayor like the actors,

or would shew respect to their lord and
master, he appoints them to play their
first play before himselfe and the Alder-
men and Common Counsell of the city;
and that is called the Mayor's play,
where every one that will comes in without money, the Mayor giving the players
a reward as hee thinks fit to shew respect
unto them. At such a play my father
tooke me with him, and made mee stand
betweene his leggs as he sat upon one
of the benches, where we saw and heard
very well." Then he gives a detailed
account of the play, which was called the
"Cradle of Security," and which is now
lost.

"Who can be so pitiless to the imagination," says Mr. Halliwell-Phillipps,
"as not to erase the name of Gloucester
in the preceding anecdote, and replace it
by that of Stratford-on-Avon?" And
who can be so pitiless to the imagination
as not to fancy John Shakespeare the
name of the mayor, and his son, the little
boy between his knees, watching the
play? We may, at all events, rest as-

sured that his son was likely to have aid-
ed in the generous welcome to the players, and the players were likely to have
remembered the intelligent lad, and tried
to requite the kindness of the father by
their hospitable reception of the son.
Who can help thinking, too, that it was
perhaps the sight of one of these old-
fashioned plays which, like young Molière's sight of the comedy at the Hôtel de
Bourgogne, first awakened in him a desire for better things than he had known,
kindled a love of poesy, and a passion
for the drama? Oh, there will come a
time when some one, some genial master
hand, will work all this up in some life-
like story, some fascinating romance,
that will charm all mankind !

Under these circumstances, nothing
can be more likely than that the magistrate's son received a generous welcome
at the hands of the actors in their London home, and that they secured him a
position in their fraternity. Besides, it
is well known that those coming from the
provincial or rural parts of England to

the great metropolis often seek out and associate with their townsmen and compatriots, who, glad to hear from home, generally receive them with kindness and favor.

Those who have resided in London know what clannishness there is, even at this day, among those hailing from the same county or town in that small island of Britain, and how generously and kindly the absentee from home takes to a new arrival from his native hills. I have seen this myself; for even as late as 1861-2, when I was in London, I was surprised to find that there were in that great metropolis associations of Yorkshire-men, Caithness-men, Welshmen, etc., expressly formed for mutual assistance and friendly intercourse. "At all events," says Mr. Halliwell-Phillipps, speaking of Shakespeare's acquaintance with Richard Field, who was a Warwickshire man, and who printed the first edition of his *Venus and Adonis,* "there was the provincial tie,—so specially dear to Englishmen when at a distance from the town of their birth,—between the Poet and his printer.". And this tie, more especially dear perhaps to a poet than to another, existed between himself and several of the actors with whom he was so long associated, and was perhaps that which drew as well as bound him to them for so many years.

It is more than probable, therefore, that he came to London with a previous understanding that he would, on his arrival, receive a position connected with the theater; for, as he was already married, and had a wife and child to support, so wise and prudent a man was not likely to have ventured to London on mere speculation. Is it likely that, if he had come to London as a sort of beggarly holder of horses at the theater-doors, he would in two years after his arrival in London have acquired sufficient wealth and reputation to become one of the fifteen proprietors of the Blackfriars' Theater? Is it likely that he would in so short a time have become the friend and companion of various noblemen and of some of the most considerable persons of the time? "The reason why we know so little of Shakespeare," says Maginn, "is, that when his business was over at the theater, he did not mix with his fellow-actors, but stepped into his boat, and rowed up to Whitehall, there to spend his time with the Earl of Southampton, and other gentlemen about the Court." The bare fact that he became the esteemed friend and companion of such men as Southampton is a proof that he was, from the first, a man of taste and refinement. So also is the circumstance that he bought, with his first considerable earnings, the finest house in his native town, and put his family into it. A man of low origin and vulgar tastes would have had other associates, and would have spent his money in quite a different way.

Instead of being incredible, therefore, Shakespeare's career seems to me of all things most credible and natural; for he came to his work in the most natural way that can be imagined. No college-bred, classic-crammed formalist could ever have composed the free and easy, precedent-defying, rule-defying, and entirely original compositions which go under his name. None but a naturally-developed, free and independent genius could have produced such marvellous works. They probably came to him as naturally and as easily as the historical romances came to Walter Scott, and he perhaps dashed off a play in as short a space of time as Scott dashed off a romance. We know this to have been the case with *The Merry Wives of Windsor*, and it is not improbable that the same was the case with others of his plays. In *Love's Labor's Lost*, he makes Biron say:

> Small have continual plodders ever won,
> Save base authority, from others' books.

"Fortunately for us," says Mr. Halliwell-Phillipps, "the youthful dramatist had, excepting in the school-room, little opportunity of studying any but a grander volume, the infinite book of nature, the pages of which were ready to be unfolded to him in the lane and field, amongst the copses of Snitterfield, by the side of the river, or by that of his uncle's hedgerows."

13

CHAPTER XIII.

SHAKESPEARE'S CAREER IN LONDON—HOW HIS CONDUCT CLOSELY RESEMBLES THAT OF THE PRINCE.

NOW let us turn to the scene in which the Prince, on ascending the throne, discards Falstaff and his other companions, and see how it resembles the Poet's conduct on arriving in London.

Enter the King and his train; the Chief Justice among them.

Fal.   God save thy grace, King Hal! my royal Hal!

Pist.   The heavens thee guard and keep, most royal imp of fame!

Fal.   God save thee, my sweet boy!

King.   My lord Chief Justice, speak to that vain man.

Ch. Just.   Have you your wits?   Know you what 'tis you speak?

Fal.   My king! my Jove!   I speak to thee, my heart!

King.   I know thee not, old man.   Fall to thy
          prayers :
How ill white hairs become a fool and jester !
I have long dreamt of such a kind of man,
So surfeit-swelled, so old, and so profane ;
But, being awake, I do despise my dream.
Make less thy body, hence, and more thy grace ;
Leave gormandizing ; know, the grave doth gape
For thee thrice wider than for other men.
Reply not to me with a fool-born jest :
Presume not that I am the thing I was ;
For God doth know, so shall the world perceive,
That I have turned away my former self :
So will I those that kept me company.
When thou dost hear I am as I have been,
Approach me, and thou shalt be as thou wast,
The tutor and the feeder of my riots :
Till then, I banish thee, on pain of death,
As I have done the rest of my misleaders,
Not to come near our person by ten mile.
For competence of life I will allow you,
That lack of means enforce you not to evil ;
And as we hear you do reform yourselves,
We will, according to your strength and qualities,
Give you advancement.—Be it your charge, my lord,
To see performed the tenor of our word.—
Set on.

When the Prince ascended the throne
he was twenty-six years of age.   When
Shakespeare came to London, and en-

tered upon his royal career as an actor
and author, he was about the same age.
This was the turning-point in his career.
He had till then but played and dallied
with the world; he now began to work.
Like the Prince, he now determined to
" plod like a man for working days," and
show those who misjudged him what
he could do, and how much they had
" looked beyond him."   He would dis-
card, banish, and shake off forever all his
wild companions and rude habits; he
would " turn away his former self " and
" live to show the incredulous world the
noble things that he had purposed."
Being now awake he " did despise his
dream," for he was " no longer the thing
he was."   All the old deer-stealing and
riotous practices became distasteful to
him, and he went vigorously to work to
learn all that his capacious mind could
grasp.   He noted the various characters
and variegated scenes in that motley
world of London, then beginning to be
the greatest center of life and intelli-
gence in Europe; studied all the best

books he could lay hands on ; began trying his hand at composition ; made his
way, step by step, from the retouching
and remodelling of old plays to the creation of new ones ; gained a footing
among his fellow-actors and authors, and
a reputation among the public, as an
excellent dramatist and a good actor ;
saved his money and sent forty pounds
(equal to two hundred pounds or one
thousand dollars of our present money)
to his father to relieve a mortgaged
estate ; and before he was thirty-three
acquired sufficient wealth to purchase the
best house in his native town of Stratford.
Like Warren Hastings at Daylesford, he
seems to have made up his mind, before
leaving Stratford, that he would recover
the ancestral estates by the exercise of
his talents, and return some day to live
in ease and comfort on them. He had
already tried his hand at verse before
leaving Stratford ; he had acquired some
literary skill in the composition of *Venus
and Adonis ;* he felt, he knew, that he
could do better ; that he could accom-

plish greater things; so he turned to the drama, not only because it was more remunerative than any other kind of composition, but because it was a more direct means of making himself felt, both among the people and among the rulers of the people. " The tide of blood in me," he says to the Chief Justice,

> Hath proudly flowed in vanity till now:
> Now doth it turn, and ebb back to the sea,
> Where it shall mingle with the state of floods,
> And flow henceforth in formal majesty.

That was his determination, and he made it good.

He now began to associate with men of rank and culture; the Earl of Southampton was his fast friend and companion; the two noble brothers, the Earls of Pembroke and of Montgomery, seem to have been his friends and patrons; he became favorably known at court, and from that time onward he was a new man altogether. Having now a wife and little ones to provide for, every motive worthy of a man called upon him to exert himself, to bring his talents into play, and to disappoint those who "did prophetically forethink his fall." Now it was he turned to books, and devoured their contents with the "divine hunger of genius"; now it was he laid all literature under contribution to supply his intellectual wants; now it was he "redeemed time when men thought least he would"; now it was his mind became "a paradise to envelop and contain celestial spirits"; now it was, in short, he was to reign in a kingdom not only greater and more glorious than any over which his predecessors had reigned, but greater and more enduring than ever king or queen had reigned over.

Even the "small Latin and less Greek" he must have acquired at this time; for how much of these could he have acquired before his fourteenth year at a village school? The fact that he knew something of these languages, having probably acquired a working knowledge of both, is proof positive of the studious and industrious turn he took at this period, and of the serious way in which he spent his time. In this very play of *Henry the Fifth*, he shows how well he knew French; and whatever other French books he may have read, there is good evidence, from a certain quotation, that he read in that language the book of books, the Geneva edition of the French Bible, 1583. That he was well acquainted with the Bishops' Bible everybody knows. I believe he ransacked libraries in pursuit of knowledge, and studied languages in order to get at their literary contents. This is proved, I think, by what Ben Jonson, his familiar friend, says of him in his famous eulogy:

Yet must I not give nature all; thy art,
My gentle Shakespeare, must enjoy a part;
For though the poet's matter nature be,
His art doth give the fashion [shape]. And, that he
Who casts to write a living line, must sweat
(Such as thine are), and strike the second heat
Upon the Muse's anvil; turn the same,
And himself with it, that he thinks to frame;
Or, for the laurel, he may gain a scorn,
For a good poet's made as well as born:
And such wert thou.   Look how the father's face

Lives in his issue ; even so the race
Of Shakespeare's mind and manners brightly shines
In his well-turned and true-filed lines ;
In each of which he seems to shake a lance
As brandished at the eyes of Ignorance.

His pages teem with allusions to literature of the best sort, and nearly all his plots are taken from well-known works of fiction in the English, French, Italian, and Spanish literatures. He had sown his wild oats; he had done with wildness and unlettered companions ; he had "broken through the clouds of ugly mists and vapors that did seem to strangle him"; and thirsting for men and things of a nobler order, he determined to make the most of that "tide in the affairs of men which, taken at the flood, leads on to fortune."

Never was such a sudden scholar made :
Never came reformation in a flood,
With such a heady current, scouring faults;
Nor never hydra-headed wilfulness
So soon did lose his seat, and all at once,
As in this king.

Could anything be more likely, from what we know of Shakespeare's life, than that he drew this picture from his own experience? Could anything be more probable, seeing that all his characters are actually drawn from life? This practice of painting one's own form and feature under another name is by no means uncommon among authors. It is, in fact, a very common practice. Has not Fielding painted himself in "Tom Jones"? Has not Dickens described himself and his early companions in "David Copperfield"? Has not Goethe given us his real autobiography in "Wilhelm Meister"? Has not Walter Scott made himself the hero of "The Antiquary," and Balzac that of "Louis Lambert"? Has not Byron painted himself in all his poems? And why should not Shakespeare, the greatest life-painter of them all, delineate himself and his companions in one of his plays? Why should not he, the greatest of realists, paint his own career in one of his delightful dramas?

There is no field like experience; there is no ground so easily described as that one has trodden one's self; there are no scenes so vivid and real to our minds as those we have witnessed in our early days ; and, consequently, there are none on which writers of fiction delight so much to dwell. Nowhere does an author walk with so sure a step as in those paths he has trodden in youth ; nowhere is he so much at home as among his early friends and companions. In fact, the best works of the great masters of fiction are generally drawn from their own life-material ; and as Fielding is at his best in "Tom Jones," Dickens in "David Copperfield," and Goethe in "Wilhelm Meister," so is Shakespeare at his best in *Henry IV.* Macaulay calls it the finest of his comedies ; and Johnson declares that "perhaps no author has ever, in two plays (*Henry IV.* and *V.*), afforded so much delight." Even in his own day it was perhaps the most highly appreciated and most popular of all his plays. "It may fairly be questioned," says Mr. Halliwell-Phillipps, "if any comedy on the early English stage was more immediately or enthusiastically appreciated than

was the First Part of *Henry the Fourth*."
There were no fewer than six editions
published in the author's lifetime, and it
became the favorite comedy, not only of
the populace, but of the Queen and the
court. There is more wit, fun, humor,
life, and philosophy in this play than in
anything else he has written. It is, as
Lord Bacon said of his confession, "his
hand, his head, his heart," his very self as
he lived. "The drama of *Henry IV.*,
taking the two parts as artistically one,"
says Mr. Hudson, "is deservedly ranked
among the very highest of Shakespeare's
achievements. The characterization,
whether for quantity, quality, or variety,
or whether regarded in the individual development or in the dramatic combina-
tion, is above all praise. And yet, large
and free as is the scope here given to invention, the parts are all strictly subordi-
nated to the idea of the whole as an historical drama; insomuch that even Falstaff, richly ideal as is the character,
everywhere helps on the history, a whole
century of old English wit and sense and

humor being crowded together and com-
pacted in him."

As I have already said, Shakespeare
no more invented men and women than
he invented plots ; he simply drew such
men and women as he was acquainted
with, and set down such conversations as
he heard around him. "Shakespeare,"
says Richard Grant White, " invented
nothing, and created nothing but character. The greatest of dramatists, he con-
tributed to the drama nothing but himself ; the greatest of poets, he gave to
poetry not even a new rhythm or a
new stanza." Character-painting was his
forte ; and surely there was no character
he knew so well and could paint so easily
as his own. "Genius is not a creator
in the sense of feigning or fancying what
does not exist," says Dr. Channing ; "its
distinction consists in discerning more
of truth than ordinary minds." Shakespeare discerned and understood the character of men and women more profoundly
than others, and he had the power of
painting them more fairly and truly than

others. Goethe says that any character that will bear examination *must* be taken from real life; and that is why every character in Shakespeare will bear the closest examination. Ben Jonson, wishing to expose a vice or a passion on the stage, built up a character to suit it: to expose avarice, he made a character avaricious in all he said, thought and did. That was not Shakespeare's way. He did not care so much to paint vices or virtues as to paint men; he thought only of the man or woman, not of the vices, and painted him or her as he or she actually was, with all the blemishes, as Cromwell wished the painter to paint him. He was the true realistic painter of the age, revealing human nature in all its shapes and forms; in its richness and its poverty; its symmetry and its deformity; its nobility and its degradation; and in so doing he found his models among the various classes of people with whom he came in personal contact.

CHAPTER XIV.

SHAKESPEARE'S LEARNING — HIS EXPERIENCE IN FOREIGN TRAVEL.

AFTER quoting various arguments by which certain writers endeavor to prove that Shakespeare read only translations, Dr. Maginn rightly exclaims, "How does all this trumpery prove that he was not able to read Plutarch in the original?" It is well known that many persons who can easily read a book in a foreign tongue prefer a translation when they can get it. Emerson declares that he never read an original when he could procure a translation. I know that, although I can read French and German almost as easily and intelligently as English, I prefer a translation of any French or German book when I can get it ; and if I wished to construct a story or an essay on the contents of that book, I should certainly study the translation in preference to the original.   The translation comes nearer home ; enters and lodges in the mind more readily ; and more naturally forms a part of one's thoughts.   Reading in a foreign tongue makes one think in a foreign way ; and perhaps one reason why Shakespeare wrote such admirable English, is because his sources were in that language, which did not prevent the natural flow of purely English words and phrases.

As to Shakespeare's knowledge of Latin, Dr. Maginn makes the very important statement, with reference to Jonson's testimony of " small Latin and less Greek," that the possession of any Greek knowledge at all in the days of Elizabeth argues a very respectable knowledge of Latin ; because at that time, it was only through Latin, and by means of no small acquaintance with its literature, that the Greek language could be ever so slightly studied.

Now if Shakespeare could read Greek and Latin, what advantage had the

university-bred men over him? The
training, the intellectual discipline, it
will be said. The training is something;
but to a mind like Shakespeare's, a
hint will do more than painful explana-
tions to another. We all know that self-
exertion is far more beneficial in education than all learning from teachers;
that, in fact, the main effort of all good
teachers now-a-days is to make scholars
teach themselves; and this is what
Shakespeare did for himself. It is well
known that most college students, after
devoting thousands of hours to the study
of Greek grammar, drop the whole subject forever. They get in at the gate of
the treasure-house, and then turn and
leave it without even glancing at its contents. Shakespeare studied Greek for
the express purpose of getting into the
treasure-house and examining its contents.
He left the grammar to pedagogues;
what he wanted was the thought, the
feeling, the sentiment, the history of the
Greeks; and these, it seems, he got. It
was not, however, his knowledge of the

14

Greek language or literature that enabled
him to do what he did; it was his innate
genius, his wonderful perception of the
character of men as he saw them about
him.   The Greeks themselves, who excelled all others in art, knew no language
but their own ; and Shakespeare would
probably have excelled all others had he
known no language but his own.

I wish to lay before the reader, in this
chapter, two remarkable passages from
good writers, showing that Shakespeare
had studied more and travelled farther
than is generally supposed.   The first,
which is from Mr. T. Spencer Baynes'
account of Shakespeare, in the " Encyclopædia Britannica," is strongly confirmatory of my view of the Poet's early
career in London ; and the second, from
Mr. C. A. Brown's book on Shakespeare's Sonnets, presents some remarkably strong arguments to show that
Shakespeare must have seen Italy.

" His leisure hours during his first year in London," says Mr. Baynes, " would naturally be devoted
to continuing his education and equipping himself
as fully as possible for his future work. It was

probably during this time, as Mr. Halliwell-Phillipps suggests, that he acquired the working knowledge of French and Italian that his writings show he must have possessed. And it is perhaps now possible to point out the sources whence his knowledge of these languages was derived, or at least the master under whom he chiefly studied them. The most celebrated and accomplished teacher of French and Italian in Shakespeare's day was the resolute John Florio, who, after leaving Magdalen College, Oxford, lived for years in London, engaged in tutorial and literary work, and intimately associated with eminent men of letters and their noble patrons. After the accession of James I., Florio was made tutor to Prince Henry, received an appointment about the court, became the friend and personal favorite of Queen Anne (to whom he dedicated the second edition of his Italian dictionary, entitled 'The World of Words'), and died full of years and honors in 1625, having survived Shakespeare nine years. Florio had married the sister of Daniel the poet, and Ben Jonson presented a copy of 'The Fox' to him, with the inscription, 'To his loving father and worthy friend Master John Florio, Ben Jonson seals this testimony of his friendship and love.' Daniel writes a poem of some length in praise of his translation of Montaigne, while other contemporary poets contribute commendatory verses which are prefixed to his other publications. There are substantial reasons for believing that Shakespeare was also one of Florio's friends, and that during his early years in London he evinced his friendship by yielding for once to the fashions of writing this kind of eulogistic verse.

" Prefixed to Florio's ' Second Fruits,' Professor Minto discovered a sonnet so superior and characteristic that he was impressed with the conviction that Shakespeare must have written it. The internal evidence is in favor of this conclusion, while Mr. Minto's critical analysis and comparison of its thought and diction with Shakespeare's early work tends strongly to support the reality and value of the discovery. In his next work, produced four years later, Florio claims the sonnet as the work of a friend ' who loved better to be a poet than to be called one,'* and vindicates it from the indirect attack of a hostile critic, H. S., who had also disparaged the work in which it appeared. There are other points of connection between Florio and Shakespeare. The only known volume that certainly belonged to Shakespeare and contains his autograph is Florio's version of Montaigne's Essays in the British Museum ; and critics have from time to time produced evidence to show that Shakespeare must have read it carefully and was well acquainted with its contents. Victor Hugo, in a powerful critical passage, strongly supports this view. The most striking single proof of the point is Gonzalo's ideal republic in *The Tempest,* which is simply a passage from Florio's version turned into

---

* Does not this look like the modesty of the Poet, who did not care to see even his greatest works in print ?—W

blank verse. Florio and Shakespeare were both,
moreover, intimate personal friends of the young
Earl of Southampton, who, in harmony with his
generous character and strong literary tastes, was
the munificent patron of each. Shakespeare, it will
be remembered, dedicated his *Venus and Adonis*
and his *Lucrece* to this young nobleman; and three
years later, in 1598, Florio dedicated the first edition
of his Italian dictionary to the Earl in terms that
almost recall Shakespeare's words. Shakespeare
had said, in addressing the Earl, 'What I have
done is yours; what I have to do is yours; being
part in all I have devoted yours.' And Florio says,
'In truth, I acknowledge an entire debt, not only of
my best knowledge, but of all, yea of more that I
know or can, to your bounteous lordship, most noble,
most virtuous, and most honorable Earl of Southampton, in whose pay and patronage I have lived
some years, to whom I owe and vow the years I
have to live.'

"Shakespeare was also familiar with Florio's earlier works, his 'First Fruits' and 'Second Fruits,'
which were simply carefully prepared manuals for
the study of Italian, containing an outline of the
grammar, a selection of dialogues in parallel columns of Italian and English, and longer extracts
from classical Italian writers in prose and verse.
We have collected various points of indirect evidence showing Shakespeare's familiarity with these
manuals, but these being numerous and minute cannot be given here. It must suffice to refer, in illus-

tration of this point to a single instance—lines in praise of Venice which Holofernes gives forth with so much unction in *Love's Labor's Lost.* The 'First Fruits' was published in 1578, and was for some years the most popular manual for the study of Italian. It is the book which Shakespeare would naturally have used in attempting to acquire a knowledge of the Italian after his arrival in London; and on finding that the author was the friend of some of his literary associates, he would probably have sought his acquaintance and secured his personal help. As Florio was also a French scholar and habitually taught both languages, Shakespeare probably owed to him his knowledge of French as well as of Italian. If the sonnet is accepted as Shakespeare's work he must have made Florio's acquaintance within a year or two after going to London, as in 1591 he appears in the character of a personal friend and well-wisher. In any case Shakespeare would almost certainly have met Florio a few years later at the house of Lord Southampton, with whom the Italian scholar seems to have resided occasionally. It also appears that he was in the habit of visiting at several titled houses, amongst others those of the Earl of Bedford and Sir John Harrington. It seems also probable that he may have assisted Harrington in his translation of Ariosto.

"Another and perhaps even more direct link connecting Shakespeare with Florio during his early years in London is found in their common relation to the family of Lord Derby. In the year

1585 Florio translated a letter of news from Rome, giving an account of the sudden death of Pope Gregory XIII. and the election of his successor. This translation, published in July, 1585, was dedicated ' To the right excellent and honorable lord, Henry, Earl of Derby,' in terms expressive of Florio's strong personal obligations to the Earl and devotion to his service. Three years later, on the death of Leicester in 1588, Lord Derby's eldest son Ferdinando, Lord Strange, became the patron of Leicester's company of players, which Shakespeare had recently joined. The new patron must have taken special interest in the company, as they soon became (chiefly through his influence) great favorites at court, superseding the Queen's players, and enjoying something like a practical monopoly of royal representations. Shakespeare would thus have the opportunity of making Florio's acquaintance at the outset of his London career, and everything tends to show that he did not miss the chance of numbering among his personal friends so accomplished a scholar, so alert, energetic, and original a man of letters, as the resolute John Florio."

After this, the reader will be ready to peruse with interest the following remarkable passage from a very clever work by Charles Armitage Brown (" Shakespeare's Autobiographical Poems," London, 1838, Bohn), proving almost to a demonstration that Shakespeare had a personal knowledge of Italy and the Italians—a passage which is quoted and endorsed by no less a scholar than Dr. Maginn in his " Shakespeare Studies ":

" I proceed," says Mr. Brown, " to show he was in Italy from the internal evidence of his works; and I begin with his *Taming of the Shrew*, where the evidence is the strongest. This comedy was entirely re-written from an older one by an unknown hand, with some, but not many, additions to the fable. It should first be observed, that in the older comedy, which we possess, the scene is laid in and near Athens, and that Shakespeare removed it to Padua and its neighborhood; an unnecessary change, if he knew no more of one country than of the other. The *dramatis personæ* next attract our attention. Baptista is no longer erroneously the name of a woman, as in *Hamlet*, but of a man.* All the other names, except one, are pure Italian, though most of them are adapted to the English ear. Biondello, the name of a boy, seems chosen with a knowledge of the language—as it signifies a little fair-haired fellow. Even the shrew has the Italian termination to her name Katharina. The exception is Curtis, Petruchio's servant, seemingly the

---

.* For a reason which the reader will see in the next chapter, let him notice that this is another proof that the first draft of *Hamlet* was an early production.

housekeeper at his villa; which, as it is an insignificant part, may have been the name of the player; but, more probably, it is a corruption of Cortese.

" Act I., scene 1. *A public place.* For an open place, or a square in a city, this is not a home-bred expression. It may be accidental; yet it is a literal translation of *una piazza publica*, exactly what was meant for the scene.

" The opening of the comedy, which speaks of Lombardy and the university of Padua, might have been written by a native Italian :

> " ' Tranio, since—for the great desire I had
> To see fair Padua, nursery of arts,—
> I am arrived for fruitful Lombardy,
> The pleasant garden of great Italy.
>   *   *   *   *
> Here let us breathe, and happily institute
> A course of learning, and ingenious studies.'

" The very next line I found myself involuntarily repeating, at the sight of the grave countenances within the walls of Pisa :

> " ' Pisa, renowned for grave citizens.' *

---

* It could hardly be expected that, while I write, a confirmatory commentary, and from the strangest quarter, should turn up on these words; but so it is. A quarrel lately occurred in Youghal, arising from a dispute about precedency between two ladies at a ball; and one of the witnesses, a travelled gentleman, in his cross-examination, gives the following opinion of Pisa: " I did not see —— in the room that night; he is now in Pisa, which I don't think a pleasanter place than a court of justice: I think it a d——d sickening place. It is much too holy for me." This was deposed to so lately as the 10th of October, 1839.—MAGINN.

They are altogether a grave people, in their demeanor, their history, and their literature, such as it
is.   I never met with the anomaly of a merry Pisan.
Curiously enough, this line is repeated, word for
word in the fourth act.   Lucentio says, his father
came 'of the Bentivolii.'   This is an old Italian
plural.   A mere Englishman would write 'of the
Bentivolios.'   Besides, there was, and is, a branch of
the Bentivolii in Florence, where Lucentio says he
was brought up.   But these indications, just at the
commencement of the play, are not of great force.

   "We now come to something more important ;
a remarkable proof of his having been aware of
the law of the country in respect to the betrothment of Katharina and Petruchio, of which there is
not a vestige in the older play.   The father gives
her hand to him, both parties consenting, before two
witnesses, who declare themselves such to the act.
Such a ceremony is as indissoluble as that of marriage, unless both parties should consent to annul
it.   The betrothment takes place in due form, exactly as in many of Goldoni's comedies :

   Baptista. . . . . Give me your hands ;
God send you joy, Petruchio ! 'tis a match.
   Gremio and Tranio.   Amen ! say we ; we will be witnesses.

Instantly Petruchio addresses them as 'father and
wife' ; because, from that moment, he possesses the
legal power of a husband over her, saving that of taking her to his own house.   Unless the betrothment
is understood in this light, we cannot account for

the father's so tamely yielding afterwards to Petruchio's whim of going in his 'mad attire' with her to
the church. Authority is no longer with the father;
in vain he hopes and requests the bridegroom will
change his clothes; Petruchio is peremptory in his
lordly will and pleasure, which he could not possibly be, without the previous Italian betrothment.

"Padua lies between Verona and Venice, at a
suitable distance from both, for the conduct of the
comedy. Petruchio, after being securely betrothed,
sets off for Venice, the very place for finery, to buy
'rings and things, and fine array' for the wedding;
and, when married, he takes her to his country-
house in the direction of Verona, of which city he
is a native. All this is complete, and in marked opposition to the worse than mistakes in the *Two Gentlemen of Verona*, which was written when he knew
nothing whatever of the country.

"The rich old Gremio, when questioned respecting the dower he can assure to Bianca, boasts, as a
primary consideration, of his richly furnished house:

> First, as you know, my house within the city
> Is richly furnished with plate and gold;
> Basins and ewers, to lave her dainty hands;
> My hangings all of Tyrian tapestry:
> In ivory coffers I have stuffed my crowns,
> In cypress chests my arras, counterpoints,
> Costly apparel, tents, and canopies;
> Fine linen, Turkey cushions 'bossed with **pearl,**
> Valance of Venice gold in needlework;
> Pewter and brass, and all things that **belong**
> To house, or housekeeping.

"Lady Morgan, in her 'Italy,' says (and my own observation corroborates her account) : 'There is not an article here described, that I have not found in some one or other' of the palaces of Florence, Venice, and Genoa—the mercantile republics of Italy—even to the 'Turkey cushions 'bossed with pearl.' She then adds, 'This is the knowledge of genius, acquired by the rapid perception and intuitive appreciation,' etc., never once suspecting that Shakespeare had been an eye-witness of such furniture. For my part, unable to comprehend the intuitive knowledge of genius, in opposition to her ladyship's opinion, I beg leave to quote Dr. Johnson : 'Shakespeare, however favored by nature, could impart only what he had learned.' With this text as our guide, it behooves us to point out how he could obtain such an intimate knowledge of facts, without having been, like Lady Morgan, an eye-witness to them.

" In addition to these instances, the whole comedy bears an Italian character, and seems written as if the author had said to his friends, ' Now I will give you a comedy, built on Italian manners, neat as I myself have imported.' Indeed, did I not know its archetype, with the scene in Athens, I might suspect it to be an adaptation of some unknown Italian play, retaining rather too many local allusions for the English stage.

"Some may argue that it was possible for him to learn all this from books of travels now lost, or in conversation with travellers ; but my faith recoils from so bare a possibility, when the belief that he saw what he described is, in every point of view, without difficulty, and probable. Books and conversation may do much for an author; but, should he descend to particular descriptions, or venture to speak of manners and customs intimately, is it possible he should not once fall into error with no better instruction? An objection has been made, imputing an error, in Gremio's question, 'Are the *rushes strewed?*' But the custom of strewing rushes in England belonged also to Italy; this may be seen in old authors, and their very word *giuncare*, now out of use, is a proof of it. English Christian names, incidentally introduced, are but translations of the same Italian names, as Catarina is called Katharine and Kate; and, if they were not, comedy may well be allowed to take a liberty of that nature."

To which Dr. Maginn adds :

"This, certainly, is ingenious, as also are the arguments drawn by Mr. Brown from *Othello* and the *Merchant of Venice;* and I understand that a later lady-traveller in Italy than Lady Morgan coincides in the same view of the case; and she is a lady* who ought to know 'How to Observe.' At all events, there is nothing improbable in assuming that Shakespeare, or any other person of cultivated mind or easy fortune—and he was both—should have vis-

---

* Harriet Martineau.

ited the famed and fashionable land of Italy. There was much more energy and action among the literery men—among men in general, indeed, of the days of Elizabeth, than of the last century; when making the 'grand tour,' as they called it, was considered an undertaking to be ventured on only by a great lord or squire, who looked upon it as a formal matter of his life. . . . . . 'In great Eliza's golden time,' the nation was not only awake, but vigorous in the rude strength of manly activity. The spirit of sea-adventure was not dead while Drake and his brother 'shepherds of the ocean' lived ; and an enthusiastic mind of that period would think far less, and make far less talk, about a voyage to the Spanish Main, than Johnson did, near a couple of centuries afterward, of jolting to the North of Scotland. The activity of Shakespeare or his contemporaries is not to be judged of by the sloth of their ancestors 'upon town,' or 'in the literary world.' It is to me evident that Shakespeare had been at sea, from his vivid description of maritime phenomena, and his knowledge of the management of a vessel, whether in calm or in storm."

Considering, therefore, how little we know of the life of the Poet, and how much he knew of the world, what scenes may he not have witnessed, what peoples may he not have seen, and what subjects may he not have studied, that we wot not of! His friend the Earl of Southampton was captain of one of the principal ships in the expedition against Spain in 1597, and afterwards had the command of a squadron under Essex. May not the Poet have accompanied him on one of his voyages? His knowledge of the Continent is too marvellously exact to have been learned at second hand. Take, for instance, the Prince's, or rather King Henry's description of French ground. The first thing that strikes one, on making a journey from England to France, is the difference in the general aspect of French soil, which looks dull and dark compared with that of England. Now mark how King Henry describes it :

> If we be hindered,
> We shall your *tawny ground* with your red blood
> Discolor.

I have been in France, and I know no word that describes its soil so exactly as this. Now which is more probable, that the Poet's knowledge came from reading travellers' books, or that it came from actual observation ? So sure as Prince Henry had seen France with his own eyes, so sure had Shakespeare. Why, France is so near to England, its coast may be descried with the naked eye from various parts of the island! And yet Mr. Donnelly thinks that the Poet never even saw the sea !

In view, too, of what Mr. Spencer T. Baynes shows of Shakespeare's early career and linguistic studies in London, and of Ben Jonson's testimony as to his studiousness and knowledge even of the dead languages, how absurd, nay how scandalous it is for Mr. Donnelly to speak of him as an ignoramus, a drunken sot, etc., etc.!

CHAPTER XV.

CONTEMPORARY REFERENCES TO SHAKE-SPEARE—HIS HOME-LIFE.

THERE was no critical literature of the stage in Shakespeare's time; but there are some references to him and his plays by his contemporaries that are exceedingly interesting. Among these is that of the dying dramatist Greene, who, when he offered his advice and warning to his literary fellow-workers, Peele, Lodge, Marlowe, and the rest, had nothing but a sneering allusion for Shakespeare. Fortunately, the ground of his dislike is obvious; and this makes his allusion all the more important. It occurs in his "Groatsworth of Wit bought with a Million of Repentance," published in 1592.

Shakespeare was at this time a dif-

15

ferent sort of man from Greene and the other roysterers; he had got beyond roystering; he had sounded the depths of folly; and having discovered its unprofitableness, had now become an earnest student, a close thinker and hard worker. Diligently yet quietly and unostentatiously laboring in his profession, he had climbed so high and gained such a prominent place in public favor, that he excited the envy of poor Greene. "Yes, trust them not," says he; "for there is an upstart crow, beautified with our feathers, who, with his tiger's heart wrapped in a player's hide, supposes he is as well able to bombast out a blank verse as the best of you; and being an absolute Johannes Factotum, is in his own conceit the only Shake-scene in the country." The expression "with a tiger's heart wrapped in a player's hide" is a parody of the line,

Oh tiger's heart wrapped in a woman's hide!

which is found in the Duke of York's speech in the Third Part of *Henry the Sixth*.

Ah, indeed! he was a Factotum, was he? Well, that shows how skilful, how industrious, how willing and useful he was! He could not only act and instruct others how to act, but he could write; he could compose plays that were better liked and more successful than even those of the learned dramatists like Greene and his fellows. Having become the leading mind in the companies with which he was connected, the actors instinctively gave way to his superior power and knowledge, and confided all to him. No doubt he gave them many a useful hint in their art; no doubt his manner was as gentle as his genius was great and his knowledge extensive; no doubt they liked his assistance in all their efforts; for though some, like Greene, were envious of him, we do not find that he had a single enemy among those that knew him intimately. Like his own Brutus,

His life was gentle, and the elements
So mixed in him, that Nature might stand up,
And say to all the world, This was a man !

Giants are always kind and considerate toward those endowed with less strength than themselves; and Shakespeare treated all his associates, even those of inferior character and capacity, with consideration, with tolerance and liberality.

But Greene did not like him.   It seems he had no personal acquaintance with the Poet, else he would have addressed him in the same familiar way in which he addressed his other acquaintances.   He knew him only by his growing reputation, and this excited his envy, especially when he found he was not one of the university set.   This successful dramatist had not, like Greene and his companions, studied at the university; he had not passed seven years within the classic precincts of Cambridge or Oxford; he had not come to town with his patrimony in his pocket, and run through it in a course of dissipation and profligacy; he had not outraged all decency, and put himself in a fair way of dying in a hospital. No; he was quite a different sort of man from this ; he avoided brawls and quarrels ; wrought steadily and soberly at his calling ; studied all he could lay hands on ; noted carefully everything he saw ; cultivated the acquaintance of the nobler sort, and observed the coarser kind of people without becoming one of them ; became the companion of gentlemen, men of rank, talent and character, wherever he found them ; acquired wealth and reputation in his profession ; relieved his father and family from debt ; bought the best house in his native town ; and lived altogether in a higher and nobler sphere than that of Greene, Marlowe, Peele, and the rest. Oh, no, poor Greene ; he was not one of your sort ; and you could not possibly like him.

"Upstart crow!" What a world of meaning there is in that phrase ! It contains a whole volume of evidence that Shakespeare was what he has ever been represented to be, one who rapidly worked himself up from a low station to one of the highest.   'Tis true, O Greene, he had not, like you and your *confrères*, taken his degree at any learned university ; tis true, he had " small Latin and less Greek "; but he had studied in a far greater university than either, that in which genius learns most : he had studied in the University of the World, and learned all about human nature ; and in this university he had taken his degree, the highest degree yet conferred upon man or woman, that of Master Mind in Literature. In this university, his teachers were the men and women who lived and toiled, loved and hated, fought and suffered by his side, from every one of whom he had learned something ; and with all his learning and ability, O Greene, he displayed one noble trait which, with you and your companions, was conspicuous by its absence : he was noted for modesty, for an humble opinion of his own merits, and for kind appreciation of the merits of others.

There is one other playwright of the day, Thomas Nash, a friend of Greene's, who makes a similar sneering allusion to

Shakespeare.   No doubt they had both, many a time and oft, in their private conferences, expressed their contempt of this "upstart crow."   This time it is not by a play on his name, but by a play on the name of one of his dramas; and the whole bitterness of the sarcasm, like Greene's, lies in its implication of the Poet's want of an education.   It occurs in an epistle to the Gentlemen Students of both Universities, prefixed to Greene's *Arcadia :* "It is a common practice now-adays, among a sort of shifting companions that run through every art and thrive by none, to leave the trade of *Noverint,* whereto they were born, and busy themselves with the endeavors of art, that could scarcely Latinize their neck-verse if they should have need; yet English *Seneca,* read by candle-light, yields many good sentences, as ' Blood is a beggar,' and so forth; and if you entreat him in a frosty morning, he will afford you whole *Hamlets,* I should say *handfuls,* of tragical speeches."

Let the reader remember that *hamlet*

means a small village or townlet, and that *Noverint* is the first word in the Latin deeds of those times, equivalent to our modern phrase, *Know all men.* The "frosty morning" is evidently an allusion to the well-known scene that thus begins :

Ham.   The air bites shrewdly ; it is very cold.
Hor.   It is a nipping and an eager air.

There are a hundred things that point to the probability that the Poet had, before he left Stratford, studied law, or passed some years, at least, in the office of an attorney. As his father, for instance, was always connected in some official capacity with the town's affairs, we may readily conceive he would be glad to have his eldest son know something of legal transactions, with which he had so much to do, and thus enjoy the benefit of his assistance in business and official affairs.

Nobody can read *Hamlet* without being convinced that the author must, at some time, have had some connection with legal business, and it is probably all the more full of law-phrases and legal allusions from the fact that the author had but recently emerged from a law office. Hence the reference to him as a *Noverint.*

" Blood is a beggar " may have reference to such sentences as these in *Hamlet :*

Your fat king, and your lean beggar, is but variable service.

To show you how a king may go a progress through the guts of a beggar.

If Nash had had the printed play before him, he would have quoted more correctly; but he evidently cited what he thought he had *heard* the actors utter. It must not be forgotten that the play was not printed at this time, and that Nash quoted what he *thought* he had heard.

Nay, more : this phrase, " could scarcely Latinize their neck-verse if they should have need," contains probably a deeper and more deadly thrust. *Neck-verse* means the verse formerly read by a criminal, claiming benefit of clergy, to save himself from being hanged. Now this may have had reference to Shakespeare's deer-stealing escapade, and his flight from the magisterial vengeance of Sir Thomas Lucy, justice of the peace. It implies, therefore, that the "shifting companion" was an unlettered criminal, a deer-stealer and fugitive from justice, who "could scarcely Latinize his neck-verse if he should have need!" Shakespeare may have been a *Noverint* or law-clerk at the time of his flight, if flight it was, and this makes the allusion all the more galling. If it were on account of this passage, I should not at all be surprised at Shakespeare's taking offence at it, as he did at Greene's allusion, which seems to have been attributed also to Nash.

In order to understand this, let us return for a moment to Greene. It was Henry Chettle who published, some time after the author's death, Greene's book, entitled "A Groatsworth of Wit, bought with a Million of Repentance;" and it seems that Shakespeare and Marlowe took offence at the publication, and demanded an apology, which Chettle made, in a tract entitled "Kind-Heart's Dream," published not long after, in these words :

"About three months since died Mr. Robert Greene, leaving many papers in sundry booksellers' hands : among others, his Groatsworth of Wit, in which a letter, written to divers playmakers, is offensively by one or two of them taken ;—and, because on the dead they cannot be avenged, they wilfully forge into their conceits a living author, and after tossing it to and fro, no remedy but it must light on me. . . . With neither of them that take offence was I acquainted, and with one of them I care not if I never be. *The other, whom at that time I did not so much spare, as since I wish I had, ... for that [him] I am as sorry as if the original fault had been my fault; because myself have seen his demeanor no less civil than he excellent in the quality he professes. Besides, divers of worship have reported his* UPRIGHT-NESS OF DEALING, WHICH ARGUES HIS HONESTY, and his facetious grace in writing, that approves his art. . . . . . I protest, it was all Greene's, not mine, nor Master Nash's, as some have unjustly affirmed."

All this looks very much like an apology for an unjust and malicious charge; and it certainly seems complete. Chettle had meanwhile made the acquaintance of Shakespeare, and had discovered how unjust and ungenerous that charge was.

Poor Nash and Greene! So you thought, like some recent critics, that the first requisite for the production of a good play, is a classic education! that none should " busy themselves with the endeavors of art" who had not received a training in the classic languages! O Envy! how blind thou art to genius, as well as to merit! Love sure never was so blind to imperfection as thou art to perfection! What a chance for a glorious, grateful immortality hast thou, Nash, lost, as well as thy boon companion Greene! And instead of being looked upon with admiration, nay with respect approaching to veneration, as the personal friends and admirers of Shakespeare, ye are now regarded as poor, pitiful, spiteful deriders of the immortal bard!

Mr. Charles Armitage Brown expresses regret that Shakespeare had not more such enemies ; for if he had, we should, he thinks, have learned by their attacks something more of him and his affairs. Perhaps we should ; but it is pleasant to know that he was almost universally loved, and that he had few or no enemies. Chettle was doubtless, like Falstaff with the Prince, "bewitched with his company," and very probably he gave him "medicines to make him love him!"*

Let me say a word here about Shakespeare's home-life. Mr. Black, in his excellent novel, "Judith Shakespeare," represents the Poet as an

---

* I am astonished that Mr. Phillipps should think, from certain references to the play of *Hamlet* as early as 1589, that these must concern an earlier *Hamlet* than that of Shakespeare. This reference of Nash's is among them, and the others are passages from the play, which are thus stated: "'There are things called whips in store,' spoken by Hamlet, and a notice of a trout with four legs by one of the other characters. Also a very telling speech by the ghost in the two words, Hamlet, revenge!" Now, how easy it would be for any spectator or listener to the play (for we must not forget that Nash simply *saw* the play, not read it), to confound Hamlet's famous speech beginning

" For who would bear the whips and scorns of time, "
with such an expression as " There are whips in store!" And as to the "trout with four legs," it probably comes from the camel that is turned into a whale:

Ham. Do you see yonder cloud, that's almost in shape of a camel?
Pol. By the mass, and 'tis like a camel, indeed.
Ham. Methinks, it is like a weasel.
Pol. It is backed like a weasel.
Ham. Or like a whale?

amiable and much-loved father, living and working entirely for his wife and children, and coming home at stated periods laden with presents and messages for his family and friends. I think he is right. There is not a particle of evidence to show that he was not well-mated in his union with Anne Hathaway, and much to show that he was.

Pol.   Very like a whale.
Ham.   Then will I come to my mother by and by.

And does not the ghost thus incite Hamlet to revenge :

Ghost.   List, list, O list !
If thou didst ever thy dear father love,—
Ham.   O God !
Ghost.   Revenge his foul and most unnatural murder !
Ham.   Murder ?
Ghost.   Murder most foul, as in the best it is;
But this, most foul, strange and unnatural.
Ham.   Haste me to know't; that I with wings as swift
As meditation, or the thoughts of love,
May sweep to my revenge !

The story or history of Hamlet was familiar enough before Shakespeare's play was written; but no other play of that name has come down to us. The first draft of *Hamlet* was in existence long before the perfected copy, first published in 1604, and described in its title-page as "enlarged to almost as much again as it was." Shakespeare was, in 1589, the twelfth among sixteen shareholders in the Blackfriars' Theater, and it is obvious that the first draft of *Hamlet* had been written and acted by this time.

His wife and daughters "did earnestly desire to be laid in the same grave with him," according to the evidence of the aged clerk, who, in 1693, showed the church at Stratford to Dowdall. "And the pleasing memorial of filial affection," says Halliwell, "in the chancel of Stratford church, a monument

---

There is no doubt, therefore, that this play, first drafted in the early years of his connection with the theater, was entirely rewritten and remodelled twenty years afterwards, when the author's mind was in its ripest stage. Byron wrote his best poem, *Childe Harold*, at twenty-four; Sheridan wrote *The Rivals* and the *School for Scandal* at about the same age; and Shakespeare was twenty-five when he wrote the first draft of *Hamlet*. To show the reader how Shakespeare worked, and the difference between his first and his second draft of a play, let me quote a few lines from *Love's Labor's Lost*, which is also supposed to be one of his earliest productions. In that play these three lines occur in the first draft:

> From women's eyes this doctrine I derive;
> They are the ground, the books, the academes,
> From whence doth spring the true Promethean fire:

which are thus gracefully expanded in the second:

> From women's eyes this doctrine I derive;
> They sparkle still the right Promethean fire;
> They are the books, the arts, the academes,
> That show, contain, and nourish all the world;
> Else none at all in aught proves excellent.

This, may, therefore, give us a good idea of *Hamlet* before it was "enlarged to almost as much again as it was."

raised by her daughter, tells us how revered was Anne Shakespeare's memory, and plainly teaches us to infer she possessed 'as much virtue as could die.' Such a being," he continues, " must have lived happily with the gentle Shakespeare." Besides, had he not been highly esteemed, he would not, in that age, have received, as an actor, such uncommonly respectful interment.

This is evidence enough that notwithstanding " the second-best bed " and all that, he lived happily with his wife. If he did not care for her, would he have invested his very first earnings in buying the best house in the town for her residence? We find him making constant journeys to and from Stratford, repeatedly buying property in that town, and finally retiring permanently there as soon as he had acquired sufficient means to live comfortably. " Let it be borne in mind," says Mr. Halliwell-Phillipps, " that Shakespeare's occupation debarred him from the possibility of his sustaining even to an approach to a continuous domestic life ; so that when his known attachment to Stratford is taken into consideration, it seems all but certain that his wife and children were but waiting there under economical circumstances, perhaps with his parents in Henley-street, until he could provide them with a comfortable residence of their own. Every particular that is known indicates that he admitted no disgrace in the irresponsible persecution which occasioned his retreat to London, and that he persistently entertained the wish to make Stratford his and his family's only permanent home." We may be sure his heart was always in Stratford ; and amid all the varied scenes in which he took part in London, the different characters he played, and the numerous persons with whom he became associated, his heart ever turned to that little town in Warwickshire

> Where were his young barbarians all at play ;
> Where was their Dacian mother ;

while he, their sire, was called hence to

make an *English holiday* for the sovereign, the dignitaries, and the people of the day.

Let any man who has wife and child, and who is obliged to go to some distant city to earn a living ; let him imagine for a moment, if he have a human heart and natural feelings, whether he too would not do all he could, work, strive, hope, fear, dream, and exert all his powers, with the view of returning to the loved ones with the means of ministering to their comfort, and pleasing them in all things.

I have not a doubt, that from the first day in which Shakespeare set foot in London, he looked forward to returning to Stratford and living there at ease with his wife and children, his parents, friends and neighbors.

> In all his wanderings round this world of care,
> In all his griefs—and God had given his share—
> He still had hopes, his latest hours to crown,
> Amid these humble bowers to lay him down ;
> To husband out life's taper at the close,
> And keep the flame from wasting by repose :
> He still had hopes,—for pride attends us still,—

Amid the swains to show his book-learned skill;
Around his fire an evening group to draw,
And tell of all he felt and all he saw;
And as a hare, whom hounds and horns pursue,
Pants to the place from whence at first she flew,
He still had hopes, his long vexations past,
Here to return,—and die at home at last!

Such is the language and such are the feelings of a poet. Indeed, not only his wife and children, but his father and mother—that dear mother, to whom he undoubtedly owed so much—were still living in Stratford, his father till 1601 and his mother as late as 1608; and it is natural that, after all the exciting scenes and tumultuous experiences of the London play-houses, he should turn, for rest and refreshment, to the quiet scenes amidst which he was reared, and to the friends of his youth and early manhood. Like the English poet already quoted, with whom he had much in common, he could exclaim:

Where'er I roam, whatever realms I see,
My heart, untravelled, fondly turns to thee;
Still to my kindred turns, with ceaseless pain,
And drags, at each remove, a lengthening chain.

CHAPTER XVI.

THE SOURCES OF THE PLAY—THE POET AND THE KING.

THE First and Second Part of *Henry IV.* being essentially one play, only too long for one representation, I shall in future speak of it as such.   Unlike some others of his plays, there is no question as to Shakespeare's sole authorship of this play.   It is true, there was before his time an old play called *Henry the Fifth*—a play which includes the events of his three plays, the First and the Second Part of *Henry IV.* and *Henry V.*—but Shakespeare seems to have been indebted to hardly a line in it for his work.   Mr. Hudson thus speaks of the old play : " The Poet can scarce be said to have built upon it or borrowed from it at all, any further than the taking of the above mentioned names. The play is, indeed, in every way a most wretched, worthless performance, being altogether a mass of stupid vulgarity ; at once vapid and vile ; without the least touch of wit in the comic parts, or of poetry in the tragic ; the verse being such only to the eye ; Sir John Oldcastle being a dull, low-minded profligate, uninformed with the slightest felicity of thought or humor ; the Prince an irredeemable compound of the ruffian, the blackguard and the hypocrite, and their companions the fitting seconds of such principals : so that, to have drawn upon it for any portion or element of Shakespeare's *Henry IV.*, were much the same as 'extracting sunbeams from cucumbers.'"

The play, therefore, is all his own, and he made full use of the freedom thus afforded him as to the nature of the characters he was to draw. I should not be surprised if, in the first draft he made of the play, he set down the real names of the persons he had in mind, and changed them afterwards for the stage.

I am supported in this view by the remarkable discoveries of Halliwell, who
shows that many of the names in these
plays are taken from those of people
living in Warwickshire in Shakespeare's
time. It looks as if Shakespeare, after
writing the play with real names, let the
names of the minor characters stand,
and changed only those of the chief
ones. Halliwell finds in the Stratford
records the names of Bardolf, Fluellen,
Davy (Jones), Perkes, Peto, Partlett,
Sly, Herne, Horne, Brome, Page, and
Ford; and he thinks it curious and
worthy of remark that "he condescended
to employ in his plays the appellations
of persons with whom he was probably
familiar in his youth." But they were
the real persons as well as the real
names. Why shouldn't they be?

" In whatever he has of historical fact,"
says Mr. Hudson, " Shakespeare's main
authority was Holinshed. And in this
case it is hard to say whether the Poet
have showed a more creative or a more
learned spirit ; there being perhaps no

other work to be named which, in the same compass, unites so great freedom of invention with so rich a fund of historical matter. Nor is it easy to decide whether there be more even of historical truth in what he created or in what he borrowed; for, as Hallam justly observes, 'what he invented is as truly English, as truly historical, in the large sense of moral history, as what he read.' "

It is worthy of remark, that the whole of the first scene in *Henry V.*, wherein the conversion of the king, his wonderful knowledge and ability, are described by the Archbishop, is omitted in the quarto editions of the play, which were the only editions published in the Poet's lifetime, and appears only in the folio edition of 1623. So that it looks as if this quiet and significant description of the character of his hero, his self-presentation of the man, were considered too tame for the boards, and left only for the closet. Or was there, perhaps, some other reason for its omission ?—It is also to be noted, that the king's speech to the

Archbishop, deprecating war, expressing great anxiety as to a rightful cause, and showing a fearful apprehension of its dire accompaniments, is greatly shortened in the quartos.

Some reader may say, "Is it not improbable that Shakespeare, an humble man of letters, should have selected a prince as one in whom to represent himself?" If there was any man in England, in this Elizabethan era, in whose breast there beat an heroic spirit, in whose mind there lived the most exalted thoughts and high-hearted hopes; if there was any man in that age accustomed to high thinking and gentle living, a born prince of men, it was William Shakespeare, the greatest of poets. Why should not this man with the chivalric name, Shake-spear, a patriotic Englishman, through whose veins flowed some of the best blood in England, see in England's heroic king a man similar to himself, loving home, peace, and social life, fond of wit, humor, and song, yet capable of heroic feats in war as well as of genial and kindly conduct in peace? Why should he not see in this king, with whose personal history he had such large sympathy, a man who had undergone an experience similar to his own, and whose character looked like his own? What is a king more than another man except that he is surrounded by ceremony? Why should he not imagine himself in his place, acting and speaking as he had acted and spoken, laughing and jesting as he had laughed and jested? He obviously saw in this Prince's history a rich field, not only for wit and humor, but for stately behavior, noble thinking, and high-hearted action; a field in which he was personally acquainted, and in which he found himself completely at home. Besides, kings were not, in those days, so far removed from the people as they are now. They often took part in public games and sports, visited the haunts of the common people, and lived and loved like other men. "I am glad thou canst speak no better English," says the king, in the wooing scene with the Princess Katharine, "for if thou couldst, thou wouldst find me such a plain king that thou wouldst think I had sold my farm to buy my crown."

Listen to what the Poet puts into the king's mouth when he, incognito, meets two or three of his own soldiers, the night before the battle of Agincourt :

King. Though I speak it to you, I think the king is but a man, as I am. The violet smells to him as it doth to me; the elements show to him as they do to me; all his senses have but human conditions: his ceremonies laid by, in his nakedness he appears but a man; and though his affections are higher mounted than ours, yet, when they stoop, they stoop with the same wing. Therefore, when he sees reason of fears, as we do, his fears, out of doubt, be of the same relish as ours are.

Could Shakespeare not stand for such a man? Does he not here show that he was man first, king afterwards? He was not a god, but a man; and being more man than most kings, being nearer the people than most princes, the Poet came all the more close to him, and had all the more resemblance to him. This view is further confirmed by what follows. One of these soldiers, who does not know it is the king, challenges him to single combat after the battle ; and, after exchanging gloves as a means of subsequent recognition, the king leaves him, and thus breaks out in a soliloquy on kings and ceremony :

King. Upon the king ! let us our lives, our souls
Our debts, our careful wives, our children, and
Our sins, lay on the king !—we must bear all.
O, hard condition ! twin-born with greatness,
Subject to the breath of every fool,
Whose sense no more can feel but his own wringing !
What infinite heart's ease must kings neglect,
That private men enjoy !
And what have kings, that privates have not too,
Save ceremony, save general ceremony ?
And what art thou, thou idol Ceremony ?
What kind of god art thou, that sufferest more
Of mortal griefs than do thy worshippers ?
What are thy rents ? what are thy comings-in ?
O Ceremony, show me but thy worth !
What is thy soul but adulation ?
Art thou aught else but place, degree and form,
Creating awe and fear in other men ?
Wherein thou art less happy, being feared,
Than they in fearing.

What drink'st thou oft, instead of homage sweet,
But poisoned flattery?   O! be sick, great greatness,
And bid thy Ceremony give thee cure.
Think'st thou the fiery fever will go out
With titles blown from adulation?
Will it give place to flexure and low bending?
Canst thou, when thou command'st the beggar's
    knee,
Command the health of it? No, thou proud dream,
That play'st so subtly with a king's repose.—
I am a king, that find thee; and I know
'Tis not the balm, the scepter, and the ball,
The sword, the mace, the crown imperial,
The inter-tissued robe of gold and pearl,
The farced title running 'fore the king,
The throne he sits on, nor the tide of pomp
That beats upon the high shore of this world—
No, not all these, thrice-gorgeous Ceremony,
Not all these, laid in bed majestical,
Can sleep so soundly as the wretched slave
Who, with a body filled, and vacant mind,
Gets him to rest, cramm'd with distressful bread;
Never sees horrid Night, the child of hell;
But, like a lackey, from sun rise to set,
Sweats in the eye of Phœbus, and all night
Sleeps in Elysium; next day, after dawn,
Doth rise, and help Hyperion to his horse;
And follows so the ever-running year
With profitable labor to his grave:
And, but for ceremony, such a wretch,
Winding up days with toil, and nights with sleep,

Hath the fore-hand and vantage of a king.
The slave, a member of the country's peace,
Enjoys it; but, in gross brain, little wots
What watch the king keeps to maintain the peace,
Whose hours the peasant best advantages.

Who will say that the imagination that conceived this could not put himself in the place of a king? Who will say that this does not look like the Poet acting and thinking in the character of a king? Perhaps no man ever realized so fully all the troubles, cares, sorrows, anxieties and duties of a king; perhaps no man ever understood so perfectly the happiness as well as the miseries of a peasant; and perhaps no man ever gave such noble expression to them. How completely he entered into the thoughts and feelings of King Henry! how completely he identified himself with him and his cares! Reading these speeches, one would think he must have been a king himself to speak in so kingly a way. But these are the thoughts of the Poet, picturing to himself how he would have spoken and acted in the place and condition of a king; or working out a life that he imagines himself to have lived. Probably no king ever addressed his troops with more hearty sympathy and true fellow-feeling than King Henry addressed his at Agincourt. He felt, what few kings ever feel, that he was one of them, an Englishman among Englishmen, and about to risk his life, like them, for his country's honor and glory:

> For forth he goes, and visits all his host,
> Bids them good morrow with a modest smile,
> And calls them brothers, friends, and countrymen.

Did Napoleon, or Blücher, or Gustavus Adolphus, or Washington, ever render his troops such tender homage? Could anything be nobler than his declaration:

> For he, to-day, that sheds his blood with me,
> Shall be my brother: be he ne'er so vile,
> This day shall gentle his condition.

Such is the noble and gentle spirit that breathes in the speech he makes to Westmoreland and his army just before the battle; which, as it is perhaps the most celebrated of all his speeches, must be given entire, and with which we take our leave of this most interesting, most amiable, and most glorious prince, whose career and character we have shown good reasons for regarding as reflecting those of the Poet himself. In reading it, let the reader call to mind that this is the man of whom it was said,. " List his discourse of war, and you shall hear a fearful battle rendered you in music ; " and remember that the same character is kept up to the end.

West. O! that we now had here

(*Enter the King.*)

But one ten thousand of those men in England
That do no work to-day !
    King. What's he that wishes so?
My cousin Westmoreland ?—No, my fair cousin ;
If we are marked to die, we are enough
To do our country loss ; and if to live,
The fewer men, the greater share of honor.
God's will ! I pray thee, wish not one man more.
By Jove ! I am not covetous for gold ;
Nor care I who doth feed upon my cost ;
It yearns me not if men my garments wear ;
Such outward things dwell not in my desires :
But if it be a sin to covet honor,
I am the most offending soul alive.

No, 'faith, my coz, wish not a man from England:
God's peace! I would not lose so great an honor,
As one man more, methinks, would share from me,
For the best hope I have.   O! do not wish one more:
Rather proclaim it, Westmoreland, through my host,
That he which hath no stomach to this fight,
Let him depart; his passport shall be made,
And crowns for convoy put into his purse :
We would not die in that man's company
That fears his fellowship to die with us.
This day is called—the feast of Crispian :
He that outlives this day, and comes safe home,
Will stand a-tiptoe when this day is named,
And rouse him at the name of Crispian.
He that shall live this day, and see old age,
Will yearly on the vigil feast his friends,
And say—To-morrow is Saint Crispian :
Then will he strip his sleeve, and show his scars,
And say, These wounds I had on Crispin's day.
Old men forget ; yet all shall be forgot,
But he'll remember with advantages
What feats he did that day.   Then shall our names,
Familiar in their mouths as household words,—
Harry the king, Bedford and Exeter,
Warwick and Talbot, Salisbury and Gloster,—
Be in their flowing cups freshly remembered.
This story shall the good man teach his son ;
And Crispin Crispian shall ne'er go by,
From this day to the ending of the world,
But we in it shall be remembered ;
We few, we happy few, we band of brothers :

For he, to-day, that sheds his blood with me,
Shall be my brother : be he ne'er so vile,
This day shall gentle his condition :
And gentlemen in England, now abed,
Shall think themselves accursed, they were not here,
And hold their manhoods cheap, while any speaks,
That fought with us upon St. Crispin's day.

I might have presented a dozen other points wherein the Prince resembles the Poet; but it is hardly necessary. Let me, however, mention two or three more. Everybody knows how fond Shakespeare is of punning. Great poet as he was, he obviously dearly loved a pun. There is not one of his plays, I think, in which he does not somewhere perpetrate a pun of some sort. Now, notice how fond the Prince is of punning! He is as good a hand at it as Falstaff himself. He twists "nave of a wheel" into "knave of a whale"; plays upon *choler*, *collar*, and *halter;* speaks of Poins's "*low countries* making a *shift* to eat up his *holland;*" and placing a dish of apple-johns before Sir John Falstaff, he tells him these are "five more Sir

17

Johns," and taking off his hat, says, "I will now take my leave of these *six* dry, round, old, withered knights!"

Has the reader ever noticed how closely the Prince observes men and things? He penetrates every man at a glance. What prince ever before deigned to notice the dress of his tavern-host as this Prince has? "This leathern-jerkin, crystal-button, nott-pated, agate-ring, puke - stocking, caddis - garter, smooth-tongue, Spanish pouch!" What prince ever before noticed so minutely the personal attire and other small matters touching his companion as this Prince has observed in Poins? "What a disgrace it is to me to remember thy name?" etc. What prince ever before noticed what the clothes of the new-born babies of struggling gentry were made of? "God knows whether those that bawl out the *ruins of thy linen* shall inherit His kingdom," etc.

Here is another point, which some might make much of. Every reader of the plays knows with what respect

Shakespeare treats Catholic clergymen and Catholic doctrines. The Church suffers no injury at his hands. One of the first among those who wrote of him ends his account by saying " he died a Papist," and certainly no one can affirm that his writings controvert the assertion. Whether he was a Papist or not, I cannot undertake to say ; certain it is, he was no contemner of the Church ; and here I find the man who most of all resembles him represented as

> full of fair regard,
> And a true lover of the holy Church ;

and so well versed in Catholic doctrine, that

> Hear him but reason in divinity,
> And, all-admiring, with an inward wish
> You would desire the king were made a prelate.

The reader may take this for what it is worth ; but I think it may fairly be looked upon as another link in the wonderful chain which has unrolled itself in my hands.

We know that Shakespeare was no

friend of the Puritans. How could he have had any sympathy with a sect that condemned all pleasure and play-acting as wicked and sinful? When he ridicules the Puritans in the character of Malvolio, and makes Sir Toby Belch exclaim, " Dost thou think, that because thou art virtuous there shall be no more cakes and ale?" he doubtless expressed his own sentiments. We must never forget that the Catholic Church, however inimical to science, has ever been the friend and encourager of art, the patron of painting, of poetry, music, and the drama, and never the enemy of social pleasure; and it is not improbable that the Poet had more sympathy with this ancient Church, which favored his art and chimed in with his inclinations, than with the new one that frowned on and condemned both as sinful.

These are things that, I imagine, cannot fail to strengthen the conviction that the Prince and the Poet are one and the same person ; and I may conclude my direct comparison, by remarking, that the sculptor who fashioned the statue of the Poet, now in the New York Central Park, formed a likeness as near that of the Prince, as the likeness of the Prince in the Poet's writings is remarkably like that of the Poet.*

---

* In view of Prince Henry's kindness toward the tapsters, his ready recognition of Falstaff's witty page, his mercy toward "the man who railed against our person yesterday," his horror of war in all its forms, his anxiety for the safety of the Harfleurians, and especially his gentle appreciation of every common soldier in his army, I do not see that Mr. Appleton Morgan is justified in his declaration, that Shakespeare had not a particle of sympathy with the people, and cared only for those of noble blood. He portrayed men as he saw them; often brutal and inhuman as they were; but he himself was never ungentle toward the lowly.

In the Poet's time, all the world thought more of the "highborn" than of the "low-born;" and it is unreasonable to expect a poet of the Sixteenth Century to be imbued with the advanced democratic sentiments of the Nineteenth. Pretty much the same kind of sentiment reigns at the present day in Germany, for even the students there have little respect for anybody except those that *are* students or *have been* students; the rest are cattle.

There is much that is interesting in Mr. Morgan's recent book, "Shakespeare in Fact and in Criticism," and his edition of Shakespeare's Plays, published by the New York Shakespeare Society, of which Mr. Morgan is President, is an admirable work; but I am inclined to think that many of his conclusions are by no means tenable. He leans strongly toward the Baconians, and exhibits anything but a reverent spirit toward the Poet.

CHAPTER XVII.

MR. DONNELLY AND HIS CRYPTOGRAM.*

WHEN somebody asked a Washington statistician to collect certain statistics for him, the first inquiry he made was, "What do you *want proved?*" This is precisely the spirit in which the Baconians have gone to work; they are not seeking for truth, or for that which facts and figures may show; but, having once conceived what they consider a plausible theory, they twist everything into facts and figures to suit this theory.

This, it may be said, is an assertion that cuts both ways; for it applies as much to my theory as to theirs. True; but will any one deny that mine is nat-

---

* This chapter was in the hands of the printer before I saw Mr. Donnelly's book. I do not find, however, anything material to change in it; and I think it worth standing as it is. The next chapter will deal directly with "The Great Cryptogram."

ural, probable, and in accordance with experience and analogy, while theirs is the contrary? Who has ever heard of such a thing as they propound? and who has not heard of such a thing as I have propounded? Had more been known of the every-day life of the Poet, his resemblance to the Prince would probably have been noticed long ago. In the spirit in which the Baconians have gone to work, you may prove anything; you may just as easily prove that Shakespeare wrote Bacon's works as that Bacon wrote Shakespeare's; you may make even figures (ciphers) lie like fiends; and things that have no more connection with each other than fire and water you may combine, and use them as wonderful evidences of the truth of your discovery. Like Macbeth's "juggling fiends," they

> Palter with us in a double sense;
> They keep the word of promise to our ear,
> And break it to our hope.

Of all the books which I have read, that which contains the most ingenious example of special pleading (let the student mark that word) is "The Authorship of Shakespeare," by Judge Holmes. This judge's performance reminds me forcibly of the astute lawyer of the olden time who declared : "Give me but three lines of any man's handwriting, and I shall send him to the gallows !" Never did lawyer, holding a brief, argue more ingeniously and skilfully to win his case ; yet never did lawyer, holding such a brief, fail more completely to convince the jury of the truth of his plea. If his book live at all, it can live only as a rare example of skill in special pleading, or as a specimen of what may be done in such pleading.

But this work seems almost unknown compared with that of another adventurer in this quixotic field, whose forthcoming work, to achieve a similar end, has been more widely heralded and more extensively advertised than perhaps any other work of this age. Perhaps no book of modern times has called forth so many leading articles, so many newspaper comments, as Mr. Donnelly's long-promised work on Shakespeare.

In the New York *World* of August 28, 1887, there appeared a thirteen-column letter by Professor Thomas Davidson, describing his visit to Mr. Ignatius Donnelly, at his home in Hastings, Minnesota, and giving the most minute account of his forthcoming book on Shakespeare, entitled, " The Great Cryptogram : Francis Bacon's Cipher in the so-called Shakespeare Plays."

Curiously enough, most of Mr. Donnelly's strange discoveries seem to have been made in these two plays (the First and the Second Part of *Henry IV.*), in which I have endeavored to show that Shakespeare portrayed his own character under the guise of that of the Prince ; and the interpretations and discoveries he finds in these two plays are more strange and startling than anything to be found in the wildest romance. On reading Professor Davidson's long and elaborate letter, I felt profoundly and sincerely convinced of one thing : that, however ingenious and skilful the discoverer, there is, for any sane man—any man capable of sound judgment—no more satisfaction in these pretended discoveries than in the ravings of a maniac.   There is not, to speak plainly, an iota of truth, or a shadow of likelihood, in the whole business.   It is one of those remarkable literary delusions, which, like the forgeries of Ireland, the discoveries of Macpherson, or the ingenious deceptions of Chatterton, are bound to disappear in time, and serve at last as a warning example,

To point a moral or adorn a tale.

To make this clear to the reader, I shall take three or four of Mr. Donnelly's propositions or discoveries, as stated by Professor Davidson, and show what far-fetched conclusions he draws from them ; and by these examples the reader may judge of the character of the rest, and of the character of the mind that advances them as proofs.

Mr. Donnelly contends that because

Shakespeare described the sea and Scottish scenery so well, he must have been to sea and to Scotland; and as we have no record of his having been at sea or in Scotland, and have a record of Lord Bacon having been at both, the latter must therefore have written the plays containing these descriptions! Because St. Albans, Bacon's birthplace, is frequently mentioned in the plays, and Stratford-on-Avon, Shakespeare's birthplace, not once, Bacon must have been the author of the plays!

Logic indeed! This reasoning reminds me of Johnson's sarcasm, "He who drives fat oxen must himself be fat!" And because the author of the plays knew so much of law, he must have been a lawyer; and what lawyer, forsooth, but Bacon! Why, according to this reasoning, he must have been a clergyman, a physician, a farmer, a soldier, a sailor, a statesman,—everything! for he knew as much of theology, medicine, agriculture, war, the sea, the state, as most clergymen, physicians, farmers, soldiers, sailors, statesmen know each of his particular profession or calling. This is what makes the Archbishop's description of him so marvellously significant and applicable: "Hear him but reason in divinity," etc. He was many men rolled into one.

It is amazing what nonsense these Baconians will write, and what nonsense these editors will print. Perhaps it is not less amazing to see how many people believe in their nonsense. I sometimes think, on seeing how many clever men accept this theory, that when a man becomes over-clever, he comes very near being a fool.

> "Great genius is to madness near allied."

To procure such stuff as this, the New York *World* sends to Minnesota a special correspondent, who talks with Mr. Donnelly, examines his work, and fills two entire pages of the paper with his discoveries, which are endorsed and believed in by Benjamin Butler and other equally able men.

As to Shakespeare's descriptions of Scottish scenery and the sea, Mr. Donnelly's assumption is not only absurd in itself, but it is absurd from the fact that there is good ground for supposing that the Poet did see Scotland and the sea. We find, for instance, that a company of English players were in Aberdeen in 1601; that they were well received and well paid; and that thirty-two marks and the freedom of the city were conferred on " Laurence Fletcher, comedian to his majesty," who seems to have been the leader of the company. Now in May, 1603, a patent was made out, by the king's order, authorizing " Laurence Fletcher, William Shakespeare, Richard Burbage," and others, to perform plays in any part of the kingdom. What is more probable than that Shakespeare was with this same Fletcher company in Scotland?—As to the sea, we know that he did travel around with a company of players; and to infer that because there is no direct mention of his having seen the sea, he never did see it,—that an actor accustomed to travel in an island "set in the silver sea," and yet never saw the sea,—is an argument worthy indeed of a Baconian mind.

In the list of the moneys received in 1592 by the Chamberlain of Stratford, the following item occurs: "Of John Shackesper for Richard Fletcher, xxs." Here is the father of Shakespeare paying to the Chamberlain of Stratford twenty shillings for a Richard Fletcher of the same town. Might not this Richard Fletcher be the father of Laurence, with whom Shakespeare was now associated as an actor and dramatist? Might not Shakespeare, while transmitting money to his father (which we know he did), be thus made the agent for a similar service to the father or kinsman of his friend and colleague? We have seen that several of Shakespeare's fellow-actors were Warwickshire men, and probably the personal friends of his father; and why may not this Laurence Fletcher be one of them? These things are, it is true, mere speculation; but they are

within the range of probability, which is
more than can be said of Mr. Donnelly's
" proofs."

We may safely conclude, from Mr.
Donnelly's absurdly unreasonable and
utterly baseless literary deductions, that
his cipher deductions are no better ; that
the stories he manufactures from the
numbers of the pages, the brackets, the
commas, the italics, the blunders in the
folio of 1623, are as fanciful and untrust-
worthy as his reasonings. Professor
Davidson confesses he can make nothing of the cipher : he tells us only
what marvellous stories Mr. Donnelly
makes out of it.

I once heard of a learned German
professor into whose hands was placed
a thick manuscript volume, said to have
been discovered among the North
American Indians by the early explorers;
and from the hieroglyphic pot-hooks,
scrawlings, and scribblings which it
contained, the professor deciphered a
whole aboriginal history of wonderful
interest ;—when, lo ! it was proved,

beyond a shadow of doubt, that the book contained nothing but the scribblings and scrawlings of a child, the son of a sea-captain, who, unable to write, amused himself during his father's long voyages by scrawling, scribbling and ciphering in this book! Mr. Donnelly's interpretations of the blunders in the folio of 1623 must have been suggested by the exploit of the German professor, for it is precisely of a piece with it. Out of the mistakes of the poor, unskilful printers of the Elizabethan era, he manufactures a marvellous story of kings, queens, princes and poets, such as none but a man of the most fertile imagination could conceive.

"The work," says Mr. Donnelly, "is vaster than I imagined. I started with an expectation of finding one or two cipher-words on each page; then I advanced to a dozen or two; then to a score or two: then I thought the cipher-words were one-fifth of the text. . . . . Now I find that more than half the words are cipher-words, and that many words are made to do double and treble duty." Is not this the very madness of midsummer? I have no doubt that he will finally end in making the whole thing, every word, a cipher, and go on finding meanings within meanings,

"in endless mazes lost,"

until he too, like Miss Delia Bacon and Mrs. Ashmead Windel, loses his wits in the mad pursuit. May not a new religion, a new bible, and a new sect, called the Cipheronians, come out of this business? What a singular fate has been that of Shakespeare,—to have first a number of spurious plays foisted on him, and then to be denied the credit of those he actually wrote! Why may not Lord Bacon, who "took all knowledge for his province," have written the plays of the other dramatists of that age, as well as those of Shakespeare? Is there no cipher in the works of Jonson, Marlowe, Greene, Lodge, and the rest? The Baconians seem to think him capable of everything, a perfectly omnipotent genius, who wrote

18

plays before breakfast, merely as a bit of recreation, before going to the serious business of the day !*

Mr. Donnelly speaks of the unaccountable loss of Shakespeare's library, manuscripts, etc.; and concludes, that because they cannot be found, he never had a library. Did not his body lie one hundred years in the grave before any notice was taken of him or his works? Was it not the Germans, not his own countrymen, who first unearthed him? One hundred years unnoticed! Mr. Buckle shows that Charles III. changed the face of Spain during his reign,—built new roads, bridges, canals, schools; remodelled the universities, encouraged literature and science, made everything new, —and yet, within less than *five years* after his death, *five* short years, everything was changed, all had vanished, and

---

* Now that the " Great Cryptogram " has appeared, I am not a little gratified to find that my own wonderful foresight is verified by the discoveries of Mr. Donnelly ; for that gentleman actually declares that Lord Bacon wrote, not only the plays of Shakespeare, but the dramas of Marlowe, the Essays of Montaigne, and the " Anatomy of Melancholy " of Burton !

every trace of his improvements was lost
forever! If five years can effect such a
sweeping change in the records of a nation, what may not one hundred years
effect in those of an individual! Although Charles had made greater changes
in Spain than had been made during the
preceding century and a half, they were
all lost, in so brief a period, because
the Spanish people took no interest in
them, did not care for them. So it was
with Shakespeare and his writings. The
people of England, after his death, lost
all interest in the drama; they went wild
on religious and political questions, and
Shakespeare and the drama were utterly
neglected; nay, suppressed; for the
Commonwealth well-nigh annihilated the
drama. It is simply by a miracle of
good luck, or rather of Providential care,
that we have even his plays, let alone his
books and manuscripts. Had his survi-
ving friends and fellow-actors, Heming
and Condell, not given us the folio edition of 1623, we should have lost most
of his plays as well as his books.

This is history; this is the language of soberness and truth; not the fanciful imaginings of a cipher-genius. " It must be borne in mind," says Mr. Halliwell-Phillipps, " that actors then occupied an inferior position in society, and that even the vocation of a dramatic writer was considered scarcely respectable. The intelligent appreciation of genius by individuals was not considered sufficient to neutralize in these matters the effect of public opinion and the animosity of the religious world; all circumstances thus uniting to banish general interest in the history of persons connected in any way with the stage. This biographical indifference continued for many years; and long before the season arrived for a real curiosity to be taken in the subject, the records from which alone a satisfactory memoir could have been constructed had disappeared. At the time of Shakespeare's decease, non-political correspondence was rarely preserved, elaborate diaries were not the fashion, and no one, except in semi-apocryphal collections of jests, thought it worth while to record many of the sayings and doings, or to delineate at any length the characters, of actors and dramatists ; so that it is generally by the merest accident that particulars of interest respecting them have been discovered."

To show how time sweeps away ordinary records, it is only necessary to notice the remarkable fact, that few men can tell anything of their ancestors farther back than their grandfathers. Stop one hundred men on Broadway, and ask each one who was his great-grandfather : and I will guarantee that ninety of them will be unable to answer. Look into the lives of great men, and you will find that few of them can go farther back than their grandfathers. Time is almost as swift and sure in destroying private records as a prairie-fire in destroying the crops of the farmer.

CHAPTER XVIII.

THE   CIPHER—ITS   FALLACY   PLAINLY SHOWN.

ON looking at this stupendous monument of labor, of ingenious and skilful labor, "The Great Cryptogram" by Mr. Ignatius Donnelly, my first feeling is one of profound regret, that so able and well-informed a man should have wasted his great powers and spent such an herculean amount of energy on so fruitless a task. Mr. Donnelly is an extraordinary man ; a man of uncommon resources of mind and tremendous energy of character. A slight acquaintance with his work will show the reader that, combined with immense knowledge, he has large imagination, great discrimination, fine powers of expression, indefatigable industry, inexhaustible faith and zeal, and boundless enthusiasm. A man of such a character may easily make something out of nothing. No task is too great for him; nothing is impossible for him; and the task he has undertaken, though accompanied by insurmountable difficulties, seems in no wise to have daunted him.

Unhappily, his zeal and enthusiasm have overbalanced and clouded his other powers: a sound judgment has been perverted by a vivid imagination, and a strong understanding has given way to a determination to succeed in a fond and foolish pursuit. He has searched so persistently, so intently, and so unrelentingly for an imaginary treasure, that he has at last forced himself into the belief that he has found it; and what he has found, though it may satisfy himself, cannot possibly satisfy any human being still possessed with the ordinary share of common sense. In short, his zeal and enthusiasm have carried him away and made him the victim of a miserable delusion.

Mr. Donnelly has discovered (we will do him the credit of thinking that he believes it himself) not only one cipher, but several, in Shakespeare's Plays. He says himself, "There are many ciphers in the plays;" and he may yet publish several books, showing a dozen or more ciphers in Shakespeare's plays. To look at his markings, notes, figures, signs, crosses, fractions, words, in different-colored inks and different-sized characters, in the folio of 1623, is enough to make one's brain reel. His work is a pyramid of industry and perseverance; none but an enthusiast, none but a man of extraordinary energy and endurance could produce such an unparalleled piece of work. In actual bulk and quantity of matter, his book would make at least a score of volumes like this. I have not a shadow of doubt—in fact the reader will soon be convinced of it himself—that the same industry, ingenuity, and perseverance, applied to the writings of any poet, would be equally productive of ciphers: Mr. Donnelly could make a cipher out of *any* book. I wonder that he has not tried his hand on Homer in the same way. What a field he would have for the exercise of his fertile imagination in the pages of the much-criticised Iliad ! If he could get hold of - an original parchment copy of that poem, he would certainly make it out as the work of Noah or of Jupiter himself !

In order that the reader may see for himself how Mr. Donnelly has gone to work, in searching for a cipher by Lord Bacon in Shakespeare's plays, I shall give him a fair sample of his book, a sample which will show not only his methods, but the spirit in which he has worked. I quote the following from "The Great Cryptogram," Book II., p. 18, omitting nothing but his foot-notes referring to the names, acts, and scenes of the plays quoted :

But it was in the first part of *King Henry IV.* that I found the most startling proofs of the existence of a cipher.

In act ii, scene 1, we have a stable scene, with the two "carriers" and an hostler; it is night, or rather early morning—two o'clock—it is the morning of the Gadshill robbery; the carriers are feeding their horses and getting ready for the day's journey; and in the dialogue they speak as follows :

> *1 Car.*   What, Ostler, come away and be hanged; come away.
>
> *2 Car.*   I have a gammon of *Bacon*, and two razes of Ginger, to be delivered as far as Charing-crosse.

This occurs on page 53 of the Histories; we have seen that the other word *Bacon* occurs on page 53 of the Comedies.   As these are the only instances in which the word *Bacon* occurs alone and not hyphenated with any other word, in all these voluminous plays, occupying nearly a thousand pages, is it not remarkable that both should be found on the same numbered page ?

We have the original of this robbery scene in another old play, entitled *The Famous Victories of Henry the Fifth*.   In each case the men robbed were bearing money to the King's treasury; and in each case they called upon the Prince after the robbery for restitution.   In the old play, Dericke, the carrier, who is robbed by the Prince's man, says:

> Oh, maisters, stay there; nay, let's never belie the man; for he hath not beaten and wounded me also, but he hath beaten and wounded my packe, and hath taken *the great rase of Ginger* that bouncing Bess . . . should have had.

But there is no bacon in *his* pack.   That was added, as in the other instances, when the play was re-written, doubled in size, and the cipher inserted.

I said that Bacon, in making any claim to the authorship of the plays, would probably seek to identify himself (as centuries might elapse before the discovery of the cipher) by giving the name of his father, the celebrated Sir Nicholas, Queen

Elizabeth's Lord Keeper; and here, in the same scene, on page 53, appears his father's name.

The chamberlain enters the stable ; also Gadshill, "the setter" of the thieves, as Poins calls him : that is, the one who points the game for them. The chamberlain says :

Cham. Good-morning Master Gads-Hill; it holds current that I told you yesternight. There's Franklin in the wilde of Kent hath brought three hundred marks with him in gold. I heard him tell it to one of his company last night at supper; a kinde of auditor, one that hath abundance of charge, too (God knows what); they are up already and call for egges and butter. They will away presently.

Gad. Sirra, if they meete not with S. *Nicholas* Clarks, Ile give thee this necke.

Cham. No; Ile none of it. I prithee, keep that for the hangman, for I know thou worship'st S. *Nicholas* as truly as a man of falsehood may.

First I would observe the unnecessary presence of the word *Kent.* Why was the county from which the man came mentioned? Because Kent was the birthplace of Sir Nicholas Bacon, and in any cipher narrative it was very natural to speak of Sir Nicholas Bacon born in Kent.

But observe how Saint Nicholas is dragged in. He is represented as the patron saint of thieves, when in fact he was nothing of the kind. Saint Anthony, I believe, is entitled to that honor. But, ingenious as Bacon was, he could see no other way to get Nicholas into that stable scene, and into the talk of thieves and carriers, except by such an allusion as the foregoing; and he made it even at the violation of the saintly attributes. Saint Nicholas, Bishop of Myra, was born in Patara, Lycia, and died about 340. " He is invoked as the patron of sailors, merchants, travellers and captives, and the guardian of school-boys, girls and children." He is the original of the Santa-Klaus of the nursery.

And in the same scene on the same column we have :

> If I hang, old *Sir* John hangs with mee.

This gives us the knightly prefix to Nicholas Bacon's name. And it appeared to me there was something here about the Exchequer of the Commonwealth of England; for all these words drop out in the same connection. Only a few lines below the word *Nicholas*, the word *Commonwealth* is twice dragged in, in most absurd fashion.

Describing the thieves, Gadshill says :

> And drink sooner than pray ; and yet I lie, for they pray continually to their saint the *Commonwealth ;* or rather not pray to her but prey on her, for they ride up and down on her, and make her their Bootes.
>
> *Cham.* What, the *Commonwealth* their Bootes ? Will she hold out water in—a foul way ?

The complicated exigencies of the cipher compelled Bacon to talk nonsense. Who ever heard of a Saint Commonwealth ? And who ever heard of converting a saint into boots to keep out water ?

And on the next page we have the word *exchequer* twice repeated :

> *Fal.* I will not bear my own flesh so far afoot again for all the coin in thy father's *exchequer*.

Again :

Bardolph.   Case ye, case ye ; on with your vizards, there's money of the King coming down the hill, 'tis going to the King's *exchequer*.
Fal.   You lie, you rogue, 'tis going to the King's tavern.

And a little further on we have :

When I am King of *England.*

And as the Court of Exchequer was formerly a court of equity, in the same scene we find that word :

Fal.   If the Prince and Poynes be not two arrant cowards there's no *equity* stirring.

Here again the language is forced ; this is not a natural expression.

All this is in the second act of the play, and in the first act we have :

As well as waiting in the *court.*
O, rare I'll be a brave *judge.*
For obtaining of *suits.*

And then we have *master of the great seal.*

Good-morrow, *Master* Gads-hill.
We'll but *seal*, and then to horse.....
For they have *great* charge.

All this is singular : *Sir—Nicholas—Bacon—of Kent—Master* of the—*great—seal* of the *Common-wealth* of *England.*

And again : *Judge* of the *court* of the *exchequer—equity.*

It is true that this might all be the result of accident.   But I go a step further.

On the *next page* 54, and in the next scene, I found the following extraordinary sentences :

Enter Travellers.

Trav.   Come Neighbor; the boy shall leade our Horses downe the hill :   We'll walk a-foot awhile, and ease our legges.

Thieves. Stay.

Trav.   Jesu bless us.

Falstaff.   Strike : down with them, cut the villains throats; a whorson Caterpillars ; *Bacon*-fed knaves, they hate us youth ; downe with them, fleece them.

Trav.   O, we are undone, both we and ours forever.

Falstaff.   Hang ye, gorbellied knaves, are you undone ?   No ye fat Chuffes, I would your store were here.   On *Bacons*, on, What, ye knaves?   Young men must live, you are Grand Jurers, are ye ?   Wee'll jure ye i'faith.

Heere they rob them and binde them.

Let us examine this.

The word *Bacon* is an unusual word in literary work.   It describes, in its commonly accepted sense, an humble article of food.   It occurs but four times in all these plays of Shakespeare, viz.:

1. In *The Merry Wives of Windsor*, in the instance I have given, page 53 of the Comedies, " Hang-hog is the Latin for *Bacon*."

2. In the 1*st Henry IV.*, act ii, scene 1, "a gammon of *Bacon*," page 53 of the Histories.

3. In these two instances last above given, on page 54 of the Histories.

So that, out of four instances in the plays in which

it is used, this significant word is employed three times on two successive pages of the same play in the same act!

I undertake to say that the reader cannot find in any work of prose or poetry, not a biography of Bacon, in that age, or any subsequent age, where no reference was intended to be made to the man Bacon, another such collocation of *Nicholas—Bacon —Bacon-fed—Bacons.* I challenge the sceptical to undertake the task.

And why does Falstaff stop in the full tide of robbery to particularize the kind of food on which his victims feed? Who ever heard, in all the annals of Newgate, of such superfluous and absurd abuse? Robbery is a work for hands, not tongues. And it is out of all nature that Falstaff, committing a crime the penalty of which was death, should stop to think of bacon, or greens, or beefsteak, or anything else of the kind.

Is it intended as a term of reproach? No; the bacon-fed man in that day was the well-fed man. I quote again from the famous *Victories of Henry V.*

John, the cobbler, and Dericke, the carrier, converse; Dericke proposes to go and live with the cobbler. He says:

I am none of these great slouching fellows that devoure these great pieces of beefe and brewes ; alas, a trifle serves me, a woodcocke, a chicken, or a capons legge, or any such little thing serves me.

John. A capon! Why, man, I cannot get a capon once a yeare, except it be at Christmas, at some other man's hous°, fo° we cobblers be glad of a dish of rootes.

Falstaff might fling a term of reproach at his victims, but scarcely a term of compliment.

But Falstaff calls the travellers *Bacons!* Think of it. If he had called them *hogs*, I could understand it, but to call them by the name of a piece of smoked meat! I can imagine a man calling another a bull, an ox, a beef; but never a tender-loin. Moreover, why should Falstaff say, "On, Bacons, on!" unless he was chasing the travellers away? But he was trying to detain them, to hold on to them, for the stage direction says: "Here they rob them and *binde them.*"

When I read that phrase, "On, Bacons, on!" I said to myself: Beyond question there is a cipher in this play.

Then Mr. Donnelly goes on to show that because the tapster's name, *Francis*, occurs twenty times, *Saint Albans*, Bacon's birthplace, several times, *Gray's Inn*, where Bacon studied, once or twice, all these are sure indications that Bacon put them there as a cipher to show "the next ages" that he wrote the plays! The repeating of the name *Francis* so often was done expressly "to draw the atten-tion of the sleepy-eyed world to the fact that there is something more here than appears on the surface!" Mr. Donnelly takes the word *white* and the word *horse*, which are five pages apart, and because each is the sixty-ninth word in the page, and the mystical number sixty-nine is the same upside down, he makes wonders out of it! One would think he had been consulting the numbers of the lottery-players, or the cabalistic terms of the spiritualist oracles, to have his head filled with such tomfoolery as this.

Wherever the word *shake* or *spear* occurs, in *any* of the plays, no matter in what connection, he draws marvellous conclusions from it. He quotes these lines, for instance, from *Henry VI :*

Who loves the king, and will embrace his pardon,
Fling up his cap, and say—God bless his majesty!
Who hateth him, and honors not his father
Henry the Fifth, that made all France to quake,
Shake he his weapon at us, and pass by :

Then jumps to *Othello*, in which Iago says:

I fear the trust Othello puts in him,
At some odd time of his infirmity,
Will *shake* this island.

Then he passes to Henry IV., where Warwick says:

19

> Peace, cousin, say no more.
> And now I will unclasp a secret book,
> And to your quick-conceiving discontents
> I'll read you matter deep and dangerous,
> As full of peril and adventurous spirit
> As to o'erwalk a current, roaring loud,
> On the unsteadfast footing of a *spear*.

Of these lines Mr. Donnelly makes much. "As a spear," says he, "did not usually exceed ten feet in length, we are forced to ask ourselves, what kind of a stream could that have been which it was used to bridge? One could more easily leap it by the aid of the spear than cross on such a frail and bending structure." When one is determined to find a cipher, how blind he becomes to poetic beauties!

Then he quotes Bardolph's account of the way in which Falstaff made his companions "tickle their noses with *spear-*grass, to make them bleed;" and asks triumphantly, "Would not *blades of grass* have done as well, without particularizing the species?" No, *blades of grass* would not have done as well; for this is one of the peculiarities of a work of genius, that the author makes his work more real by particularizing.

Then he turns again to *Henry VI.*, where the Duke of York says:

That gold must round engirt these brows of mine;
Whose smile and power, like to Achilles' *spear*,
Is able with the change to kill and cure:

and then remarks: " This comparison of a man to a spear, and a medicinal spear at that, is not natural." If anything is not natural, it is surely Mr. Donnelly's interpretations. He might as well quote the following from Ecclesiasticus to prove that Shakespeare or Bacon wrote the Bible:

"Thy alms shall fight for thee against thine enemies better than a mighty shield and strong spear." Ch. xxix., v. 13.

Does the reader want any more of this stuff? Is there, in literature, anything so absurd as work of this kind? But this is not all. I *must* quote a little more, to show the extraordinary lengths to which he can go:

In a great many instances the word *Bacon* seems

to have been made by combining *bay* with *con*, or *can*, which in that day was pronounced with the broad accent like *con*, as it is even yet in England and in parts of America.

In such a desperate *bay* of death.—*Richard III.*
The other day a *bay* courser.—*Timon of Athens.*
To ride on a *bay* trotting horse.—*King Lear.*
I'd give *bay* curtail.—*All's Well That End's Well.*

He seems to have been fond of the bay color in a horse.

Why, it hath *bay* windows.—*Twelfth Night.*
The *bay* trees are all withered.—*Richard II.*
Brutus, *bay* not me.—*Julius Cæsar.*

And then we have :

Ba, pueritia, with horn added. *Ba.*—*Love's Labor's Lost.*
Proof will make me cry *ba.*—*Two Gentlemen of Verona.*

And when we come to the *con*, it is still more forced :

Thy horse will sooner *con* an oration.—*Troilus and Cressida.*

The cipher pressed him hard when he wrote such a sentence as this.   It is not the horse will *deliver* an oration, or the horse will *study* an oration ; but the horse will *con* it.

And again :

But I *con* him no thanks for it.—*All's Well That Ends Well.*
Yes, thanks, I must you *con.*—*Timon of Athens.*

I should say the cipher did "press him hard" to induce him to write such nonsense.   Could anything under heaven be more far-fetched ?

But in order to expose the fallacy of his arithmetical cipher, I shall make one more quotation from his book, and then I am done with him forever:

Being satisfied that there was a cipher in the Plays, and that it probably had some connection with the paging of the Folio, I turned to page 53 of the Histories, where the line occurs:

I have a gammon of BACON and two razes of ginger.

I commenced and counted from the top of the column downward, word by word, counting only the spoken words, until I reached the word BACON, and I found it was the 371st word.

I then divided that number, 371, by fifty-three, the number of the page, and the quotient was seven! That is, the number of the page multiplied by seven produces the number of the word *Bacon.* Thus:

$$53 \times 7 = 371$$

This I regarded as extraordinary. There are 938 words on the page, and there was, therefore, only one chance out of 938 that any particular word on the page would match the number of the page.

But where did that *seven* come from which, multiplying 53, produced 371 = *Bacon?* I found there were seven italic words on the first column of page 53, to-wit: (1) *Mortimer* (2), *Glendower* (3), *Mortimer* (4), *Douglas* (5), *Charles* (6), *Waine* (7), *Robin.*

There are 459 words on this column, and there was, therefore, only one chance out of 459 that the number of italic words would agree with the quotient obtained by dividing 371 by 53.   For it will be seen that if *Charles Waine* had been united by a hyphen, or if *waine*, being the name of a thing, a wagon, had been printed in Roman letters, the count would not have agreed.   Again, if the word *Heigh-ho* (the 190th word) had not been hyphenated, or if *Chamber-lye* had been printed as two words, the word BACON would not have been the 371st word. Or if the nineteenth word, *infaith*, had been printed as two words, the count would have been thrown out.   If *our selves* (the sixty-fourth and sixty-fifth words) had been run together as one word, as they often are, the word *Bacon* would have been the 370th word, and would not have matched with the page. Where so many minute points had to be considered, a change of any one of which would have thrown the count out, I regarded it as very remarkable that the significant word *Bacon* should be precisely seven times the number of the page.

Still, standing alone, this might have happened accidentally.

I remembered, then, that other significant word, *Saint. Albans*, in act iv, scene 2, page 67, column 1.

And the shirt, to say the truth, stolen from my host of *S. Albones*.

I counted the words on that column, and the word *S. Albones* was the 402d word.   I again divided this total by the number of the page, 67, and the quotient was precisely 6.

$$67$$
$$6$$
$$\overline{}$$
$$402 = \text{“ S. Albones.”}$$

I counted up the italic words on this column, and I found there were just *six*, to wit : (1) *Bardolph* (2), *Peto* (3), *Lazarus* (4), *Jack* (5), *Hal* (6), *John*.

This was certainly extraordinary.

There were on that page 890 words. There was, therefore, but one chance out of 890 that the significant word *S. Albones* would precisely match the page. But there was only one chance in many thousands that the two significant words *Bacon* and *S. Albones* would both agree precisely with the pages they were on ; and not one chance in a hundred thousand that, in each case, the number of italics on the first column of the page would, when multiplied by the page, produce in each case numbers equivalent to the rare and significant words *Bacon* and *S. Albones*.

Now, all this looks plausible ; at least some may think it looks plausible ; but a little examination will show that there is a fatal falsity in the whole proceeding which at once destroys his conclusions. When he does not succeed by dividing the number of words by the *number of the page*, he divides by the number of *italic* words; when this does not succeed, he divides by the number of *hyphens;* when this does not succeed, he divides by the number of *parentheses;* when this does not succeed, he divides by the number of *brackets;* when this again does not succeed, he divides by a *certain number of lines;* when this does not succeed, he divides by *something else;* and when this fails him, he *multiplies*, or *adds*, or *subtracts* anything he fancies. If, in counting the words one way, he does not succeed, he counts them in another; if beginning at the top of a column will not do, he begins at the bottom; if this will not do, he begins at the middle; if this again will not do, he begins at the end or at the beginning of a scene, or anywhere he chooses! He says himself (and the wonder is, that he should confess such a thing, and expect people to believe in his cipher): " After a long time, by a great deal of experimentation, I discovered [*discovered* is good!] that the count runs not only from the beginnings and ends of acts, scenes, and columns, but also from the beginnings and ends of such sub-divisions of scenes as are caused by the stage directions, such as 'Enter Morton,' 'Enter Falstaff,' 'A retreat is sounded,' 'Exit Worcester and Vernon,' 'Falstaff riseth up,' etc."

Does not this beat anything ever conceived? Is it fair? Is it just? Is it philosophic? Can the man believe in it himself? One would think that, either he had lost his wits, or he must think that other people have lost theirs. Surely there is a screw loose in some part of his capacious brain, or an obliquity cast in his mental vision, which prevents him from thinking logically, or seeing straight and clear, as other people think and see. I fail to see an iota of reason, of common-sense, of probability, in the whole business; and to me, not the least wonderful part of it is the circumstance, that so shrewd and capable a man as Mr. Donnelly should have worked himself into a belief in it.

I now see (May, 1888) that the critics
are nearly unanimous in condemning Mr.
Donnelly's cipher. Even Professor Davidson says :* " I am now convinced (and
I say this with the utmost regret, for Mr.
Donnelly's sake) that he is entirely mis-
taken in thinking that he has discovered
a cipher in the plays. The cipher breaks
down," he continues, "just where I suspected it would. It follows no single
definite principle ; it is *capricious*. Its
author sets out, in every case, by *deter-
mining what he wishes to find*, and then
exercising his ingenuity in reaching it by
a calculation always containing an element of caprice. . . . . All the coher-
ency in Mr. Donnelly's curious results is
due to *arbitrary counting*."

The long-dreaded "cipher discovery"
is now, therefore, completely exploded,
and "The Great Cryptogram" will be
relegated to the huge collection of fail-
ures, hoaxes, and delusions of the past.

The following paragraph from the pen
of the able London correspondent and
literary critic of the *New York Tribune*,

Mr. George W. Smalley, may suitably close the whole cipher controversy :

" Mr. Donnelly's 'Great Cryptogram' published in London to-day (May 2, 1888) receives the honor of a long obituary notice in *The Standard*. Mr. Donnelly had indeed prepared for his own funeral by once more refusing to disclose the key of the 'Cryptogram.' He had previously delayed on the plea that he should lose his copyright, and now again postpones it on the pretext that he wishes to work it out in more plays. But it does not matter. His present reviewer, who writes with signal fairness, admits that Mr. Donnelly's literary argument, though not original, is a solid and conscientious piece of literary criticism. But to the 'Cryptogram' he is merciless. One of Mr. Donnelly's most important root numbers, 523, which he professes to have obtained by multiplying certain unnamed numbers, cannot have been obtained by multiplying any numbers whatever. The cipher, on examination, proves to be nothing more than a system so flexible and so arbitrarily used that anybody can make any story with it that the words in Shakespeare supply. There is just show enough of method to deceive those who do not examine details. But Mr. Donnelly is the author of his own story, selecting his words in the first instance and framing a sort of arithmetical justification for them afterward. The story itself is but a tissue of trivialities. Such is this reviewer's sentence.

"Finally Mr. Charles Athill Bluemantle, Pursuivant-of-Arms in the Heralds' College, publishes a statement that he has examined the original papers relating to the Shakespeare grant of arms. There can, he affirms, be no doubt that a patent was assigned to Johan Shakespeare, father of the poet, in 1596, which was ratified in a subsequent assignment for Arden. There is ample proof that the grantee established the fact that he was of sufficient social position to warrant the issue of the patent. This letter, as the reviewer well says, is a crushing blow to much of the matter of the cipher, and to all the theory of Mr. Donnelly's book."

CHAPTER XIX.

SOME IMPORTANT CONSIDERATIONS TOUCH-
ING THE BACONIAN THEORY.

THE Baconians cannot get over the circumstance that Shakespeare should have thought so much of money-getting, of real estate speculations, of his rank as a gentleman, and so little of his writings. How little these critics seem to know of the history of men of letters! There is nothing more common than this among men of this class. Did not Walter Scott think much more of his rank as a Scottish nobleman, of his position as a gentleman of landed estate, the head and founder of a family, than of all his fame and influence as an author? Did not Congreve think much more of his rank as an English gentleman than of his wide reputation as a wit and dramatist? and did not Voltaire tell him he would not have thought it worth while visiting him if he were merely a gentleman ? Did not Swift confess that his highest ambition was to ride in a coach and four, and be able to say " Damn you " to any man living ? Shakespeare saw, as Swift did, the immense respect, the solid comfort and independence, which rank and wealth enjoyed in England ; and it is natural that he should have looked upon the attainment of these as the *ne plus ultra* of worldly ambition. He had indeed been painting and praising men of noble blood all his life, and it was natural that he should now aspire to be one of them himself.

It is a remarkable fact, one which Shakespeare has no doubt somewhere noted himself (for everything may be found in his writings), that men of genius generally think more of some inferior quality which they possess, or at which they are aiming, than of that by which they are distinguished. This is one of their weaknesses ; and it is plain, from what we know of the pains taken by Shakespeare to "gentle his condition," that he thought much more of the rank he held as a citizen of Stratford than of that which he held in the eyes of the world as an author and actor. Mr. Halliwell Phillipps rightly thinks, that Shakespeare's "continued increase of property in the neighborhood of his early home had constant reference to the establishment of a family, which should for ages inherit the fruits of his exertions." Did not Scott's efforts have the same object? and was not Scott, of all men, the one man who, in genius, character, and productions, came nearest to Shakespeare?

It has been asked, How should Shakespeare, with his plebeian training and associations, have acquired such knowledge of the language, manners, and conduct of the nobility, as he displays in the historical plays? I might ask in reply, How should Bacon, with his patrician training and associations, have acquired such knowledge of the language, manners, and conduct of the commonalty, as is displayed in these same plays? The poet, the man of imaginative power, is much more likely to form correct notions of unknown territory, than the philosopher, the man of facts, figures, and logical conclusions. I have heard that Dumas, before he ever saw Italy, described that country much more correctly and graphically than any traveller that had seen it. This is the power of genius; this is that magical power which we call imagination, and which plodders cannot comprehend.

But Lord Bacon was also a man of genius, with uncommon powers of imagination. True; but poetry was not his forte; he did not live, move, and have his being in the regions of fancy, but in the regions of fact. He was a logician, an expounder of principles, a pathfinder in science, a practical philosopher, whose grand aim was *utility*, the finding of things of practical usefulness to mankind. Now this is the very opposite of Shakespeare's character. While Bacon aimed to improve the physical and social condition of men, Shakespeare strove to fill their souls with joyful or sad feelings, to inspire their minds with noble fancies, high thoughts and heroic aspirations. Besides, how should Lord Bacon, the companion of refined and noble people, the studious, serious, and learned nobleman, the philosophic Christian and practical moralist, who declared that he "was born in an age when religion was in no very prosperous state," and wished to rise to civil dignities in order that, by the exercise of his talents, he "might effect something which would be profitable for the salvation of souls,"—how should this man have fallen in love with such a reprobate as Falstaff, and have made him a leading character in three different plays? Does not every one who is at all familiar with his writings feel that such a thing is contrary to reason, to analogy and experience? A hen cannot lay ducks' eggs, nor a hound give birth to foxes.

On the other hand, any one who is at all familiar with the life of Shakespeare,

20

such as it is, can see nothing remarkable in his being familiar with such men as Falstaff, Pistol, and Bardolph, and loving to portray them. Not only among the motley crowds of the London taverns and public-houses ; not only among the hangers-on at the theaters and places of public resort, but even among the Stratford roysterers, such characters are likely to have been among his familiars.*

Apart from his lack of ability for such a piece of work, Bacon's whole life, which is well known for its serious aims, forbids us to suppose he could have had a hand in the creation of such a character as

---

* Mr. Spencer T. Baynes has discovered some remarkable things that show how easily this may have been the case. As late as 1592, when the poet's father was still in difficulties, "it is officially stated, as the result of an inquiry into the number who failed to attend the church service once a month, according to the statutory requirement, that John Shakespeare, with some others, *two of whom, curiously enough, are named Fluellen and Bardolph,* 'come not to church for fear of process for debt.'" Dickens drew his father and his mother in Micawber and his wife. Is it not possible that Shakespeare drew *his* father and mother in one or more of his plays? Why not ? If we could only get behind the scenes, we might find that we know really more about Shakespeare and his family than we do about many a man with a two-volume biography.

Falstaff. The practical, scientific, experimental, Christian philosopher, who spoke of himself as "a servant of God," and all of whose writings breathe morality, soberness, and utilitarian wisdom, never could have given himself up to the creation of such a "villanous, abominable misleader of youth," such a "white-bearded Satan," as Falstaff. He would have thought he was, instead of "effecting something profitable for the salvation of souls," demoralizing the youth of the country, by creating such a character. Bacon's writings are not distinguished for wit and humor, but for wisdom and sagacity, for "wise saws and modern instances;" whereas Shakespeare and his characters, especially in the comedies, are the very embodiment of wit and humor, fun and frolic, bent upon fooling and being fooled "to the top of their bent!" Bacon labored to educate man socially, and to improve his material condition; Shakespeare labored to amuse and instruct him, to lighten his cares and enliven his spirits, to "fill his eyes with

pleasure and his ears with melody." He
endeavored to soothe the troubled and
care-worn spirit with wit and laughter;
to amuse the toil-worn artisan and
anxious courtier by the exhibition of joy-
ous carelessness and rash venturesome-
ness; he strove to shame the idler and
the sluggard by setting before his eyes
his country's heroes toiling and moiling
for fame and honor.   To do this well, he
ransacked the literature of Europe; he
read not only all the best histories,
the best legends, ancient and modern,
but all the light, romantic tales of
France, Italy and Spain, the famous old
legends of popular heroes and heroines
of Britain, and the lives of patriots, mar-
tyrs, and statesmen everywhere.   Charles
Reade, on finding that Shakespeare borrowed so largely from all sources, used
to call him, irreverently but significantly,
"the great Warwickshire thief!"

What interest could Bacon find in all
these light tales and amorous romances?
Were not such studies foreign to his
tastes, as displayed by his writings?

Shakespeare, like the bee, could extract honey from them all; he was the great alchemist who could transmute base metals into gold; and so, indeed, could Bacon, but for very different purposes. Each followed the bent of his genius; each worked for different objects; precisely as those do who read their writings. Imagine William Cobbett composing a five - act play! Imagine Charles Mathews or Theodore Hook writing a long, serious discourse on taxes!

"To ask me to believe," says Mr. Spedding, the well-known biographer of Lord Bacon and editor of his works, addressing Judge Holmes, whose book, "The Authorship of Shakespeare," he says he has read from beginning to end,—"To ask me to believe, that a man who was famous for a variety of other accomplishments, whose life was divided between public business, the practice of a laborious profession, and private study of the art of investigating the material laws of nature,—a man of large acquaintance, of note from early manhood, and one of the busiest men of his time, but who was never suspected of wasting time in writing poetry, and is not known to have written a single blank verse in all his life —to ask me to believe that this man was the author of those plays, that is to say, of fourteen comedies, ten historical dramas, and eleven tragedies, exhibiting the greatest, and the greatest variety of excellence that has been attained in that kind of composition,—is like asking me to believe that Lord Brougham was the author, not only of Dickens' works, but of Thackeray's and of Tennyson's besides." Now, if Mr. Spedding thought thus—a man who made a life-study of Bacon's works and who thoroughly understood the character of his mind and the events of his life—how absurd it must be for any ordinary reader of Bacon to credit him with the writings of Shakespeare !

While nothing in Bacon's life and writings, therefore, justifies us in supposing that he was familiar with the lives and manners of the rough-and-ready characters that abound in Shakespeare's plays, Shakespeare's life and writings show us that he was familiar with such characters, and knew all about them. It is generally allowed that Shallow and Silence were characters such as he had known and associated with in and around Stratford. Who were Mouldy, Shadow, Wart, Feeble, and Bullcalf but poor country clodhoppers, such as he had often seen and spoken to in the same region? Who were Pistol, Poins, Bardolph, and Mrs. Quickly, but people such as he had seen in the taverns of London and elsewhere? And why not Falstaff as well as the rest? Were such people Lord Bacon's familiars? We are sure they were not; for, from the nature of the man, he could take no pleasure in their conversation, and would be the last person in the world to affect their company.

How did Molière, the son of the old-clothes dealer, learn the language and manners of the nobility of France? Probably he had no better opportunity of becoming acquainted with the noblemen of the court of Louis XIV. than Shakespeare had with those of the court of Elizabeth.   Not only the Earl of Southampton, but William, Earl of Pembroke, and Philip, his brother, Earl of Montgomery, seem to have been the personal friends and patrons of Shakespeare : witness the words of Heming and Condell, who dedicated the first complete edition of his works to these two last-named noblemen : "But since your lordships have been pleased to think these trifles something heretofore, and have prosecuted both them, and their author living, with so much favor ; we hope that (they outliving him, and he not having the fate, common with some, to be executor to his own writings) you will use the same indulgence towards them you have done unto their parent." They showed "indulgence" toward the Poet; that is, kindness and friendship, as expressed in the language of the time. How little they imagined how greatly they honored themselves by this friendship !

I have already quoted Maginn's saying : " The reason why we know so little of the Poet is, that when his business was over at the theater, he did not mix with his fellow-actors, but stepped into his boat and rowed up to Whitehall, there to spend his time with the Earl of Southampton, and other gentlemen about the Court." Why should it be surprising, that a man so surrounded, so befriended, and so enriched, should have learned the language and behavior of gentlemen, and have tried to become one of them himself?

The operations of genius, which are so mystical to others, are sometimes not perfectly explicable to the man of genius himself. When Hogg's publisher objected to some of his poems because he could not understand them, the poet indignantly replied : " Hoot, man, I dinna understand them mysel sometimes!" I doubt whether Shakespeare could tell, for instance, how he became so intimately acquainted with the heart of woman. He would probably say he divined it. By a sort of sixth sense, combined with large common-sense, he succeeded in portraying her character so truly. Mrs. Siddons, the most majestic of Shakespearean actresses, declared that he seems to have known every feeling, every thought, every wish that enters a woman's heart. How absurd to bring an accusation of ignorance against such a man! If he knew the very inmost heart and nature of woman, and could express her feelings, thoughts, and wishes so admirably, how much more those of his own sex, no matter of what rank? The genius of Shakespeare could surely mount into the region of nobility much more easily than the genius of Bacon could descend, dramatically, into that of the commonalty; and it is much more likely that Shakespeare, the student of human nature, should have acquired this marvelous insight into the thoughts and feelings of woman, than Lord Bacon, the sober student of syllogistic and practical philosophy.

Shakespeare is all action, life, and poetry ; Bacon is all contemplation, calmness, and repose ; Shakespeare all imagination, wit, and humor ; Bacon all logic, science, and sense. "As far as we know," says a writer in *Temple Bar*, "it would have been as impossible for Lord Bacon to portray character in action as it would have been foreign to Shakespeare's mind to have reasoned from propositions to a logical system."

CHAPTER XX.

BEN JONSON, BACON, AND SHAKESPEARE.

IT is well known that Lord Bacon engaged Ben Jonson to turn some of his philosophical writings into Latin, and the great philosopher treated the learned dramatist so well, that the latter ever spoke with respect and esteem of him. I have sometimes thought, what a pity Jonson did not avail himself of his acquaintance with Bacon to introduce his brilliant friend Shakespeare to him, and afterwards give an account of the interview! What a delicious bit of reading that account would be! What editor would not give a thousand dollars for a report of that conversation! I have no doubt each would have richly enjoyed the conversation of the other. But whither am I straying? Very probably some of the Baconians will say that this is how Shakespeare became acquainted with Bacon, and came into the possession of the plays! There is no telling what absurdities they may not commit.

Now, if Bacon were really a dramatic author, writing such plays as his admirers suppose he wrote, is it likely that he would never have spoken of his plays, never have counselled about some passage, scene, or character in one of his plays, with the recognized dramatic authority of the day, the "big gun" of the stage, the famous dramatist whom he thus employed and knew familiarly in a literary way? And if he did so, is it likely that Jonson would never have mentioned the fact? If he were the author of the plays attributed to Shakespeare, is it credible that honest Ben would have given Shakespeare the sole and entire credit for them, and eulogized him in the boundless way he did? Is it not monstrous to suppose that this downright, outspoken, fearless man had turned conspirator, and acted such an

outrageously false and perfidious rôle as
the Baconians imagine? Consider for a
moment what Ben Jonson, who was well
acquainted with the life and works of
Shakespeare, wrote of him :

> Soul of the age,
> Th' applause, delight, the wonder of our stage,
> My Shakespeare, rise !   I will not lodge thee by
> Chaucer or Spenser, or bid Beaumont lie
> A little further, to make thee room :
> Thou art a monument without a tomb,
> And art alive still while thy book doth live,
> And we have wits to read, or praise to give.

And then, after showing how he out-
shone Lily, Kid, and Marlowe, and
though he had "small Latin and less
Greek," did far surpass the poets of "in-
solent Greece or haughty Rome," he
continues :

> Triumph, my Britain ! thou hast one to show,
> To whom all scenes of Europe homage owe.
> He was not of an age, but for all time !
> And all the Muses still were in their prime,
> When, like Apollo, he came forth to warm
> Our ears, or like a Mercury to charm.
> Nature herself was proud of his designs,
> And joyed to wear the dressing of his lines;

Which were so richly spun, and woven so fit,
As since she will vouchsafe no other wit.
The merry Greek, tart Aristophanes,
Neat Terence, witty Plautus, now not please;
But antiquated and deserted lie,
As they were not of Nature's family.
Sweet Swan of Avon! what a sight it were
To see thee in our waters yet appear;
And make those flights upon the banks of Thames
That so did take Eliza, and our James!

Could there be any higher praise? Could there be any fuller or better appreciation of Shakespeare's genius? Could this be written of one who never wrote the plays, Jonson and all the actors of Shakespeare's companies having been duped and deceived by Shakespeare? Could Jonson so write, if there were a shadow of suspicion that he was not the author of the plays?

Then, again: if Jonson, the learned Greek and Latin scholar, appreciated the self-taught Shakespeare so highly, surely there must have been others who appreciated him just as highly; and if he were so highly appreciated, even by the learned of his day how could Bacon be ashamed of claiming the authorship of such works, if they were his? or how could Shakespeare take such works from Bacon and palm them off as his own? Mr. Donnelly claims that the knowledge of such authorship would be fatal to Bacon's political prospects. Could anything be more absurd? If Bacon were the father of the plays, he would rather throw his political prospects to the winds than disown or deny such offspring.

Ben Jonson knew the man and his works; he knew both Bacon and Shakespeare, and knowing both, he could not have been deceived, nor could he deceive. He knew how Shakespeare studied; how he toiled, how he wrote, and what he wrote; he knew the character and genius of the man, which no lover of the Poet ever appreciated better than he; and remembering how admirably he conducted himself, and what a pleasant companion he was, he cherished and loved his memory as a friend, as much as he admired and venerated his

genius as a poet. Knowing and esteem-
ing Lord Bacon as he did, loving and
admiring Shakespeare as he did, is it
for a moment to be imagined that he
went deliberately to work to pervert
the truth, mock the dead, falsify the
living, and deceive posterity for all
time? Such an idea is so monstrous, I
am almost ashamed to ask the question.

"You will not deny," says Mr. Spedding, addressing Judge Holmes, "that
tradition goes for something; that, in
the absence of any reason for doubting
it, the concurrent and undisputed testimony to a fact of all who had the best
means of knowing it, is a reason for believing it, or at least for thinking it more
probable than any other given fact which
is irreconcilable with it, and which is not
so supported. On this ground alone,
without inquiring farther, I believe that
the author of the plays, published in 1623,
was a man named William Shakespeare.
It was believed *by those who had the best
means of knowing*, and I know nothing
which should lead me to doubt it." This

is sane reasoning, conclusive I think, to those who think sanely.

In his Apology, Lord Bacon speaks of having written a sonnet (he adds, quite naturally, "though I profess not to be a poet"), tending to a reconciliation between Queen Elizabeth and the Earl of Essex; and this sonnet he says he showed to one of the Earl's friends, "who commended it." Is it conceivable that the man who could thus take a pride in showing a sonnet he had composed, and in mentioning the fact that it was favorably regarded by a friend, should have written the most superb tragedies and comedies the world ever saw, and never once, in speech or in writing, have spoken of them to any living soul ?

We know that Shakespeare died in 1616, and that his last play was written before 1612; we know that Bacon lived till 1626—ten long years after Shakespeare's death—and that his last years were passed in perfect ease and quietness. Why, if he were fond of dramatic composition, did he not compose, after

Shakespeare's death, at least one more of those Shakesperean plays of which he is supposed to be the author? Why, in the name of all that is reasonable, did he not, in the ripest, wisest, most experienced, and most leisurely part of his life, throw off one of those divine dramas that must now have come so easy to him? Every proof, every sign, every vestige of evidence, every reasonable suspicion falls to the ground.

The folio of 1623 is crammed with errors and blunders of every kind; while Bacon's own works are perfectly correct im every particular: not a comma misplaced, nor a blunder of any kind, is to be found in them. How comes it, then, that these are faultless, while the plays are bristling with errors? How comes it that these prose writings are so carefully corrected, while the poetical ones are not? Surely no sane person can fail to see that this is simply because the author of the latter was dead, and could not correct the printed proofs of his works; while the author of the former was living, and carefully corrected all he wrote before going to press.

If the plays were Bacon's, how could he have allowed them to be collected by the friends and fellow-actors of the dramatist (1623), prepared for publication, and printed with all manner of errors, interpolations, and blunders as the plays of Shakespeare? Nay, more; allowed them to be printed with laudatory verses and eulogiums on the spurious author, from various well-known hands, among them one from his friend Ben Jonson! How could he have allowed those plays to be thus published, with the highest praise of the man who was not the author, and without a word of comment from him? To those who make such ridiculous assertions, I can only reply, in the words of Antony:

O Judgment! thou art fled to brutish beasts,
And men have lost their reason!

CHAPTER XX.

CONCLUSION.

THE whole Baconian theory is so preposterous, I am almost ashamed to say another word about it ; but now that I am at it, I shall endeavor to finish it. A hundred things might be said to show its absurdity ; but I will content myself with but two or three more, which, I think, together with those arguments I have already given, will be sufficient to settle the matter forever.

It is contended that because there are many expressions and thoughts in Shakespeare's writings that are to be found in Bacon's, these must have been written by the same hand. In this way, one might prove almost any writer of that day to have been the author of Shakespeare's plays. Nay, one might prove that some

writer of the present day, or of the day
before Shakespeare, was their author.
There is nothing new under the sun.
The very words I am now using, the very
sentence I am now writing, and possibly
every sentence in this book, may, in
some shape, be pointed out in some other
author.   We are all of us constantly bor-
rowing words and expressions one from
another, or unconsciously repeating what
was uttered before.   In every age, certain thoughts and certain expressions are
more or less predominant; and to argue
that because one literary man uses in his
works expressions or thoughts similar to
those of another, these must have been
all written by the same hand, is the
height of absurdity.   By such reasoning,
anything, as I said, may be proved.
Proved?   Why, has not somebody
proved, or pretended to prove, that our
Saviour never existed?   Did not Berkeley prove that there is no such thing as
matter ?   Anything may be proved, after a
fashion; and I have no doubt that somebody will, in the next generation, prove

that Shakespeare never existed at all.
But as a matter of fact, even this kind of
"proof" can by no means be allowed.
If anybody should know the style of
Bacon as compared with the style of any
of his contemporaries, that man is Mr.
Spedding, who was familiar with almost
every line that Bacon wrote. Now hear
what this gentleman says of these similar expressions, these parallelisms, collected by Judge Holmes: "Shakespeare
may have derived a good deal from
Bacon: he had no doubt read the 'Advancement of Learning' and the first
edition of the 'Essays'; and most likely
had frequently heard Bacon speak in the
Courts and the Star Chamber. But
among all the parallelisms which you
have collected, with so much industry,
to prove the identity of the writers, I
have not observed one in which I should
not myself have inferred, from the difference of style, a difference of hand. . . . .
I doubt whether there are five lines together to be found in Bacon which could
be mistaken for Shakespeare, or five

lines in Shakespeare which could be mis-taken for Bacon, by one who is familiar with the several styles and practiced in such observation." Then he goes on to show that style, like the hand-writing of different persons, is something which, though apparently similar on a superficial examination, is found to be altogether different on a close examination.

It is painful to see how Shakespeare has been dragged down into the dust by some of the Baconians, Now that they have fallen foul of him, and found him out to be an impostor, there is nothing too odious they can say of him: he is an ignoramus, a deceiver, a drunken sot, a mere money-grabber; and so on.

> O mighty Poet! Dost thou lie so low?
> Are all thy conquests, glories, triumphs, spoils,
> Shrunk to this little measure?

When Berkeley proved that there is no such thing as matter, Byron said it was no matter what he said; and when the Baconians prove that Bacon wrote

Shakespeare's plays, and that Shakespeare was an illiterate ignoramus who could hardly sign his own name, etc., it is no matter what they say, we are not going to heed them. If there were no madness in the world, sanity would not be properly appreciated.

In his last will and testament, Lord Bacon gave particular directions as to the disposal of his books and manuscripts; and in this document occurs the well-known sentence: "For my name and memory, I leave it to men's charitable speeches, to foreign nations, and to the next ages." Now, if he had been the author of the plays, is it at all likely, is it in any way conceivable, that he would have left them unmentioned, unregarded, in this important document? Did they contain such deadly thrusts against government that, like Junius, he feared vengeance on his descendants, of whom he had none? Did these plays, that so "did take Eliza and our James," contain such deadly treason? Or will any sane man maintain that

Bacon was unaware of their merit, and thought them too poor to own? Even if he were afraid of the verdict of his own generation—which, as we have seen, was universally favorable—he could certainly have left them without apprehension, like his "name and memory," to "the next ages." But it seems absurd to argue the question any further. Had it not been for the scantiness of the materials for Shakespeare's life, nobody would ever have dared to raise a doubt concerning his right to what went under his name; and had it not been for the scantiness of these materials, his delineation of himself, and of other well-known characters in his plays, would probably have been noticed long ago.

Bacon had done a great life-work in other spheres. He was an active lawyer and politician, a courtier and constitutional adviser of the Crown, a judge of the highest court in England, an original and profound investigator of natural phenomena, and a voluminous miscellaneous writer. He had crowded the work of several lives into these spheres alone ; and surely his activity in all these various occupations, all of them more or less congruous, is sufficient, without making him out a great dramatic poet as well, a quality altogether foreign to his character ; and crediting him with the work of another life, the greatest, but one, of all the lives that ever were lived. "That a human being," says Mr. Spedding, " possessed of the faculties necessary to make a Shakespeare should exist, is extraordinary ; that a human being possessed of the faculties necessary to make a Bacon should exist, is extraordinary ; that two such human beings should have been living in London at the same time, . is more extraordinary still ;—but that one man should exist possessing the faculties necessary to make *both*, would have been the most extraordinary thing of all." I should think so ; so extraordinary that it is simply impossible.

Besides, has anybody ever heard of a dramatic author writing a play,—nay, thirty-seven plays,—which he never desired to see acted, or in the proper presentation or printing of which he never took any interest whatever? No such author ever existed; no such man ever existed. Bacon was a man who sought power and influence in everything he did; and even if he had had the ability to write the plays, it is childish to suppose he would not have made the most of them. Not only the king and queen, the courtiers and the foremost men of the time, but all the nobility of England, would have been at his feet; and he would never have been obliged, in order to live respectably, to sue for assistance at court, or to marry the daughter of a London alderman.

Still more: there are Bacon's letters; letters addressed to various persons and on all manner of subjects; letters of friendship and letters of business; letters on state affairs and letters on domestic affairs; letters on literature and letters on philosophy. Surely, if he had written the plays, some mention of them would

have been made in some of these letters;
surely either he or his correspondents
would have had something to say about
them. But no; not a word on the subject is to be found. He could not have
been such a god as to have written the
plays without knowing it himself; hardly
a divinity could do that; yet I have
no doubt some of the Baconians are
capable of believing something of this
sort, for this is about as reasonable as
the rest of their logic. Like Columbus
he discovered a new continent, and
added a new world to literature, without
knowing it!

There is his intimate friend Hobbes, a
voluminous writer, who knew him well,
and who has a good deal to say of Bacon:
indeed, he might have known equally
well Shakespeare himself,—for his life
covered nearly a whole century, 1588–
1679;—yet he has never a word to say of
Bacon having written a play, or of his
having had any connection with the stage.
Hobbes was his secretary, I believe, for
a time; he wrote, examined, and studied

for him; so if any man ought to know something of his master's writings, he ought; and if any man would have mentioned the fact, had his master devoted himself to play-writing, he would have done so.

Bacon lived, in fact, in the white heat and bright light of public life; he kept a great house, and had many servants, secretaries, dependants, and friends; his acts were universally known and criticised; and to imagine that such a man, under such circumstances, should have written the finest dramas ever composed, thirty-seven in number,—dramas that were acted during twenty odd years, before the *élite* of the world,—without anybody knowing or suspecting, not even himself, that he was the author of them, is simply to the last degree preposterous and absurd.

One word more, and I have done. Does the reader remember how Lord Bacon came to his death? He was riding along in his coach one stormy winter day, when, seeing the ground covered with snow, he began to wonder whether snow would not preserve flesh from decay ; and stepping out of his coach into a poultry-shop, he bought a fowl, and with his own hands stuffed it with snow. This operation brought on a chill ; and feeling ill, he was compelled to stop at the house of a friend, Lord Arundel's, where, being put into an unaired bed, he contracted a fever, of which he died. Now let any man, tolerably familiar with Shakespeare's dramas, imagine for a moment whether the author of *Hamlet* and *Lear* was likely, on observing the ground covered with snow,—

> beautiful snow,
> Filling the sky and the earth below,
> Over the house-tops, over the street,
> Over the heads of the people you meet,
> Flying to kiss a fair lady's cheek ;
> Clinging to lips in a frolicsome freak !
> Beautiful snow ! from the heavens above,
> Pure as an angel and fickle as love !

let him imagine, I say, for a moment, whether the author of these plays would at such a sight, engage in speculating

as to whether snow would preserve
dead chickens from decay, and actually stop and stuff one with his own
hands to see if it would remain un-
tainted! Would not the mind of Shakespeare have been engaged in reflections
of quite a different nature? The action
of Lord Bacon was quite in keeping
with his character as a practical utilitarian philosopher; but it was entirely
out of keeping with the nature of the
speculative, dreamy, castle-building character-studying Poet. Shakespeare, it is
true, hit upon great physical truths by
poetic inspiration; but he hardly went
to work to find them out by actual
experiment. He was more interested,
naturally, in human character, in human
aims and hopes, in beauty of expression,
in the power of thought and example,
than in the discovery of useful truths
in natural science.

These considerations may not, it is
true, influence the views of any man
who is bound to be singular in such matters; but to one who is accustomed to

rational thinking and reasonable conclusions, they must form a chain of evidence, strong as links of iron, in proof
of the fact that the author of Shakespeare's plays and that of Bacon's philosophical works are not, and can not be,
one and the same person, We may,
therefore dismiss the subject with the
assurance, that notwithstanding the wide-
spread plot to destroy Shakespeare's
reputation and to erase his name from
literature, he "still lives," and will con-
tinue to live, as long as the language
lives in which his immortal works are
written.   Like the Prince in whom he
portrayed his own character,

> he still survives,
> To mock the expectation of the world,
> To frustrate prophecies, and to raze out
> Rotten opinion, who hath writ him down
> After his seeming.

22

INDEX.

339

WORTHINGTON COMPANY'S
NEW PUBLICATIONS.

NEW PREFACE, NEW EDITION, NEW PLATES.

TAINE (H. A.). History of English Literature. Translated by H. VAN LAUN, with introductory essay and notes by R. H. Stoddard, and steel and photogravure illustrations by eminent engravers and artists. 4 handsome octavo vols., green or blue cloth, white labels, $7.50.

TAINE (H. A.). History of English Literature. With introductory essay by R. H. Stoddard. 4 octavo vols. in two, cloth, white label, $3.75.

EDITION DE LUXE OF

A TREASURY OF ENGLISH SONNETS. Edited from the original sources, with notes, by DAVID M. MAIN. Illustrated with steel portraits. 1 vol., royal 8vo, 11½ x 7½ x 2, 470 pages, $7.50.

ALAEDDIN AND THE ENCHANTED LAMP. Zein Ul Asnam and the King of the Jinn. Two stories done into English from the recently discovered Arabic text, by JOHN PAYNE, of the Villon Society. (The concluding volume to and uniform with Payne's Arabian Nights.) 1 vol., 8vo, vellum, $7.50. Limited to 500 copies.

"JUBILEE EDITION."

FESTUS. A Poem. By PHILIP JAMES BAILEY. With beautiful steel plates by Hammitt Billings. Beautifully printed. 4to, cloth gilt, $3.50. Full gilt and gilt edges, $5.00.

THE BANNER LIBRARY.

A collection of the best works of fiction by British, French, and American authors. In 12mo volumes. Each, in paper, 25 cents.

1. My Good Friend. ADOLPHE BELOT.
2. Jane Eyre. BRONTE.
3. East Lynne. Mrs. WOOD.
4. Last of the Mohicans. COOPER.
5. Willy Reilly. CARLETON.
6. John Halifax. MULOCH.
7. Adam Bede. ELIOT.
8. Harry Lorrequer. LEVER.
9. Handy Andy. LOVER.
10. Bristling with Thorns : A Tale of the South. BEARD.
11. Won by Waiting. LYALL.
12. The Reproach of Annesley. GREY.
13. The Silence of Dean Maitland. GREY.
14. Old Mam'sell's Secret. MARLITT.
15. Airy Fairy Lilian. By the DUCHESS.
16. Nora's Love Test. M. C. HAY.
17. The Two Chiefs of Dunboy. FROUDE.
18. We Two. EDNA LYALL.
19. Five Weeks in a Balloon. By JULES VERNE.
20. Afloat in the Forest. By Captain MAYNE REID.

Others in preparation,